FLIGHT PATH

MELISSA F. MILLER

1

Eighteen months ago
The Offices of Thomas Workman, M.D.
Carlisle, Pennsylvania

Mike sank back in the soft leather chair and stared at his old friend, waiting for him to tell him what he already knew. Tom scrubbed a hand over his scalp, rifling his close-cropped white hair. Then he sighed, rested his forearms on the mahogany desk that separated them, and leaned forward.

"Mike ..." he began, then paused.

"We've known each other a long time, Tom. Don't beat around the bush."

Mike's doctor and long-time golf partner grimaced. "I think you must know. It's not good news."

Mike pressed his lips together and nodded. He'd had an inkling. And when Tom suggested meeting in his office to go over his test results instead of subjecting Mike to the indignity of a paper gown and a freezing metal exam table, that had been the confirmation.

"I'm dying."

Tom let his eyes close for an instant, then he opened them and met Mike's gaze unwaveringly through his wire-rimmed glasses.

"Yes."

Even though Mike had known, his heart ticked up a beat. He caught his lower lip between his teeth, then he rested his elbows on his thighs and interlaced his fingers.

"My lungs?"

"Your lungs. Silicosis."

Tom reached up and turned on his large wall-mounted monitor, then tapped a button on his computer. An image from Mike's most recent chest x-ray appeared on the screen. Tom opened Mike's chart with a bit too much force and the metal paper holder affixed to the top banged hard against the polished desktop.

Mike stared at the picture on the monitor. It was all shades of black and gray. It looked like nothing. But it felt like something every time he drew a deep breath or coughed or climbed a flight of stairs.

"Okay," he said just to say something.

"I don't know how I missed it. I've been looking for it forever, monitoring. I've gone back over the past five years of films. As recently as last year, it was mild. *So mild.* There was no indication that it would progress like this. That's not how it happened with your father or your grandfather."

Mike blinked at that. "You checked?"

"I ordered their charts up from the practice archives. My uncle Gus treated both of them, you know that?"

He shook his head. He hadn't known.

"Both of them followed the same pattern. Chronic silicosis. Slow progression, developing after twenty years or more of exposure in both cases. Then a gradual five-year slide. A typical track for moderate exposure."

Mike glanced over at the picture of his lungs uncomprehendingly. "This is different?"

"Yes. I don't understand how it advanced so quickly. It should have taken another decade for you to start feeling the effects. To need prescription steroids or maybe supplemental oxygen."

Mike's mind flitted to his old man's bronchodilator, always at his elbow, especially toward the end.

"So, I need to take steroids? Get an inhaler?"

Tom didn't answer but asked a question of his own, the raw anger in his voice giving way to curiosity, "You implemented the safety procedures we talked about, right?"

"Yeah, years ago. When my dad retired. The air filtering, the N95 masks, the cleaning, all of it."

Tom shook his head. "And you're the CEO for crying out loud. You're not working on the line."

"No, but I did. For years." His father had insisted he learn the business from the ground up.

"Sure. That's why we've been monitoring you. But, Mike, this goes beyond an accelerated case. It's ... acute. It came on hard, and fast. There's no treatment for this. It's too late for a lung wash, and you're not a candidate for cellular therapy. I'm ... I'm sorry. I can keep you comfortable, steroids and an inhaler might work for a while. Maybe supplemental oxygen. But the best I can do is try to get you on a transplant list. I'm sorry." Tom's medical veneer slipped, and he choked out the words.

Mike leaned forward to place a comforting hand on his doctor's arm. "It's not your fault, Tom, you did everything right."

"I can't understand it," he said more to himself than to Mike.

For a moment, Mike considered telling him about the secret project he'd been working on after hours. How he'd grind and polish after the line shut down and the teams went home, working late into the night. He hadn't run the filtering system, because it was noisy and he didn't want anyone to know what he was doing. But he *had* worn a mask—usually.

He caught himself before he blurted out the confession and said, "Sometimes things happen, Tom. You're a good doctor, and you've been a good friend."

Tom's Adam's apple bobbed, and he cleared his throat. "Do you want me to call your daughter? Have her come get you?"

"No, don't bother her. I drove myself here, I'll

drive myself home. In fact, please don't mention this to her."

"You know I wouldn't. Criminy. Anyway, it's against the law. HIPAA."

"Sure, right. Could I just ... have a minute?"

"Take all the time you need." Tom clapped a heavy hand on Mike's shoulder and headed out of his own office to give Mike some privacy.

Tom was halfway out the door when Mike said, "So a year?"

"If you're lucky. Two if you're damned lucky."

"If I'm not?"

"Three months, maybe."

"Well, I guess I'm gonna have to be lucky at least until the Club opens for the season. I can't go to my grave without beating you on the back nine one more time."

Tom laughed, and it seemed almost genuine, then the light flickered out of his eyes, his shoulders rounded, and he pulled the door closed behind him.

As the latch clicked softly into place, Mike dropped his forehead into his hands. Months wasn't enough time. Not enough time to finish the project and secure his legacy. To make the little company that his father's father started in 1944 a true international powerhouse.

His shoulders shook as he sobbed soundlessly.

He was close. So damned close. And he was going to fail. How was he going to secure his family's place in history and take care of his daughter now? He'd had it all planned out. Now, he was going to need to take a different path.

2

Present Day
Pittsburgh, Pennsylvania

Bodhi squatted in the garden and pulled the weeds from the earth methodically and at an unhurried pace. With each thorny thistle he dug out of the soil, he was mindful that he was giving nutrients and life to the tender green shoots by removing the choking weeds. And the seedlings would give back to him with herbs and vegetables and, if his luck held, plump, juicy berries.

He wiped his brow with a dirt-streaked glove then stood to stretch and crack his back. He surveyed his work. The vegetable plot was done. Now all he had left to weed was the wildflower garden he'd planted along the back fence. The flowers felt indulgent, but they were important. The riotous blooms in their bright colors brought joy to everyone who walked through the alley. Most of all the neighborhood kids, who loved to see the giant sunflowers peering over the top of the fence to turn their bright yellow faces to the sun.

He smiled at the thought as he walked over to the potting shed to exchange his trowel for a pair of pruning shears. His head was bent over the canvas tote that organized his tools when he heard Mrs. Parsons and Ms. Ingle chatting away as they took their daily stroll around the neighborhood, their arms pumping and their ponytails bobbing. He raised his hand in greeting and was about to call out a hello when the breeze carried Georgina Ingles' sharp tone over the fence.

"I told her that we don't want that kind around here."

"You *didn't*, Georgie."

The two women stopped walking and faced off.

"I did. She wants to rent her house, that's fine. But she should consider the feelings of the other people on this block. The ones who have to live next to her riffraff."

Lolly Parsons clicked her tongue. "Riffraff?"

"Oh? You don't agree? What word do you want me to use? Trash?"

"Georgina!"

"Oh, it's all well and good for you to be high and mighty. Your house is paid off. I can't afford to be underwater on my mortgage if property values drop."

"You don't need to worry about that. Property values are skyrocketing. Ever since those tech companies moved in the market's been hot. That couple on the corner sold their little dumpy place for half a million dollars."

"Oh, they did not."

"They *did.*"

"Well, then she should sell instead of renting it out. And if you think I'm wrong to say so, well, we'll have to agree to disagree," Georgina sniffed.

"You know." Lolly said slowly, "Chad Loveland *did* say someone broke into his truck last week. Stole his E-Z pass and some pocket change."

"You see?" Georgina demanded with a ring of triumph.

Bodhi edged back into the shed before they noticed him, eager to avoid the sharp gossip and ill will flowing like poison off the tongues of the women in the alleyway. He stayed behind the potting shed, concealing himself until they turned the corner.

As he walked toward the flower bed, he thought about how cynical and hard his neighbors were. Unkind.

It wasn't until he'd crouched to examine the flowers that he realized he was no different—standing there, in his garden, judging them.

He frowned. It wasn't the first time he'd done it. His own cynicism, his inability to see the good, to feel compassion, lovingkindness for his fellow humans rose up to confront him. All he seemed to see was wickedness.

You're off your chosen path.

He took a deep breath, rolled his neck, and returned to his task of weeding. The plants needed nourishment and care. He could consider his path later. Now, tend to the flowers. He was brushing mulch off some bright green daffodil shoots, when the thought materialized.

It's the work.

Could it be? He'd gone to medical school for the same reason most people did—to help others. But once there, he discovered he wanted to help the dead, not the living. To bear witness to their stories, honor their lives, and treat them with dignity and care in death. And, for many years, he had.

But once he'd become known as a forensic pathologist with an aptitude for ferreting out dark secrets and evil motives, his work had changed. The cases he consulted on exposed him to so much murder and greed and hatred. It was an irony that he had chosen a right livelihood, the fifth factor of the noble eightfold path, in keeping with the requirement to choose an occupation that would do violence to no one. And yet it was harming someone —it was harming him.

The clarity was as bright and sudden as the sun bursting through heavy clouds on a gray day.

His mind was weed-choked. His heart was withered and dormant. He needed to tend to his garden by clearing out the decay and debris so that he could see the good in the world once more.

He finished his task, then packed up the garden implements and returned them to the shed. He went into the house, washed his hands at the sink, and dried them with a kitchen towel. Then he took a sip of cool water and pulled out his phone to call Bette. There was no point in putting it off.

She answered on the second ring. "Chief Clark."

He raised a brow, puzzled by the formal salutation and crisp demeanor. “It’s me.”

He heard the creak of her chair and then the soft click of her office door closing.

“I know it’s you. I just had the mayor and one of the councilmen in my office. I could hardly say hey, ‘hot stuff.’”

He chuckled. “Is this a bad time?”

“No, it’s a great time. They were lingering, saying their goodbyes, and the ringing phone moved them right along. Johansson’s walking them out. So, please tell me you’re calling to say you’re getting in a day early.”

He swallowed.

“Bodhi?”

“I’m not going to be coming out this weekend after all.”

“A new case.” Her tone was resigned, accepting of the notion that he would interrupt their time together for a crime.

Of course, she was the chief of police. She would do—and had done—the same, many times.

“No, it’s not a case.”

“Oh?”

“It’s a personal matter.”

There was a long pause. “Is this a business call?”

"No."

"Well, then, I guess it's a personal call."

"I suppose it is."

"So you can share your personal matter. Unless it's a secret?"

He grimaced. "No, it's not a secret. I just need to spend some time alone."

"Are you saying you don't want to see each other anymore?" She was probing, testing.

"No, that's not what I'm saying. I'm saying I need to take some time alone to think about some things."

When she spoke next, her voice was firm but careful. "We talked about this. When you're in a relationship with a person, you talk to them."

She was right. They had talked about it. And he had agreed to do so. He searched his mind for the words to explain why he needed to be alone. The memory of the way he'd hurt Eliza Rollins with his careless words of wanting to be alone so many years ago reared up in his mind like a great fanged snake. Right speech was a necessity here.

"Are you there?"

"I am. I'm trying to think of the proper way to say this."

"The proper way is to spit it out."

"No. I don't want it to come out wrong."

"Fine, I'll interrogate you. Do you need to be alone to think about us?"

He could answer this. "No. It's not about us."

"Ah, the old it's not you, it's me claim."

"Actually, yes. Well … it's not me, not exactly. It's my place in the world."

"Your place in the world?" she echoed.

"I can't find the good anymore, Bette, because all I see is the bad. Evil. The depravity of human nature. You, of all people, must know what I'm talking about."

"Ah." He heard the telltale click of her pen as she tapped it against her teeth. It signaled that she was deep in thought. After a moment the clicking ceased. "I get it. I do see the worst in people. But I also get to see the best in people—because I serve the living, and they can change. If I arrest some punk kid for petty theft, it might be the wake-up call that puts him on the right path. All you can do is put people in the ground."

"Right."

"But finding the cause of death is doing good. You've helped bring closure to families and justice to killers."

"I used to think that was a helpful thing to do.

And it may be, on balance. But the darkness is poisoning my mind."

"So are you saying you're not going to do forensic consulting anymore?"

"I'm not sure. That's why I need to go somewhere alone—to figure it out."

"A silent retreat sort of deal. You could do that here, you know. The Prairie Zen Center's right in town."

"I can't. You'd be too ... there'd be too many distractions."

A hint of amusement colored her voice. "Distractions, huh?"

"Yeah. Besides, isn't there a new moon this weekend? I'm sure the Onatah Astronomy Club is getting together."

She laughed her husky laugh. "I'm a big girl. You don't have to come up with a way for me to entertain myself in your absence. So, go off and contemplate your place in the world and examine your nature. Take the time you need. But just know that you have someone to talk to about this stuff. You can talk to me."

"I know. And I will," he promised. "But before I can talk to you, I need to listen to me."

3

Wingman's Saloon
Norfolk, Virginia
Thursday
just before midnight

Crystal trailed a fingernail around the condensation beading up along the outer rim of her cocktail glass. The crowded bar was humid, thanks to a combination of body heat and an underpowered air-conditioning system, and her caipirinha was sweating as much as she was. And she was sweating plenty. The trickle of moisture ran down her neck, through the hollow of her collarbone, and pooled in her bright pink halter top.

She lifted her heavy hair from the nape of her neck and twisted it into a thick mass of curls. Less come-hither than the long loose locks she'd spent nearly an hour perfecting, but the breeze across her bare neck was worth it. Besides, he'd already noticed her. It wouldn't be long now.

She lifted the drink to her lips and sipped it, delighted when a sliver of melting ice slid down her throat. She sensed him approaching on her right and tilted her head to the left.

He leaned in over her right shoulder and tapped two fingers on the scarred, sticky bar. He smelled of soap and cedar.

"Hey, Ace, another beer," he called to the grumpy, balding bartender, raising his voice just loud enough to be heard over the frenetic drums of the live band being ignored in the corner. He dropped an empty bottle on the bar.

The bartender nodded. The man turned his head toward Crystal, fast, like an owl noticing a mouse.

"And get the lady a fresh mojito."

"Caipirinha." Crystal and Ace the bartender corrected him in unison.

He raised his palms, *my bad,* and smiled broadly. "Caipirinha, then. Is this seat taken?"

She hooked her stiletto heel around the base of the stool and pushed it out. No, it wasn't taken. She'd used a combination of death glares and blocking techniques to keep it that way just for this occasion.

"It is now." She gave him a slow smile.

He mounted the stool and stuck out his right hand. "Red Serrano, Naval Aviator."

She pumped his hand up and down, eyeballing his buzz cut. "I'm Crystal. Red, huh? Hard to tell, but you don't look like a ginger to me."

He dropped her hand and ran his palm over his shorn scalp. "Yeah, no. My hair's dark brown when it grows in. Red's a joke. The name's Reid. Reid Serrano. Serrano, like the red-hot pepper. Reid Pepper, Red Pepper. Get it?"

She laughed. "Got it."

Ace slid a fresh cocktail glass and a frosted beer across the bar and scooped up the old ones. "Red's being modest. He's also a top-notch fighter pilot. The squadron gave him the call sign 'cause of the pepper thing, but also they say he's the Red Baron reincarnated."

Red laughed, but Crystal noted the gleam of pleasure in his eyes.

"Wow, you're a fighter pilot?" She pitched her voice high and breathy.

"Yes, ma'am."

She leaned in closer and raised the glass to her lips. "That must be so exciting. What's the most dangerous mission you've ever flown?"

He grinned, and the skin around his eyes crinkled. His arm looped casually around the back of her barstool and his hand brushed against her bare back as he launched into his story. She shivered at his touch and smiled into her glass. Red Serrano might think he was the owl and she was the mouse.

But she knew better. She was the spider. He was the fly.

Friday

Very early, before dawn

Red propped himself up on his elbow and watched her fly around the motel room's dim bathroom. She pulled on her clothes, dragged a brush through her tangled hair, and squeezed some of the complimentary toothpaste onto her finger. She ran her finger across her teeth then cupped her hands under the water to rinse her mouth.

She spat in the sink and met his eyes in the mirror. "Don't you have to get going? Report to base or whatever?"

He gave her a lazy smile. "Nah, I'm off-duty today." He patted the bed and raised his eyebrows.

"That's nice, but I'm not. I have to get to work."

He rolled over and eyed the clock. "At four in the morning? You a shift worker?"

"No. I have to go back to Pennsylvania. I'm just down here consulting on a project."

"Consulting, huh? What do you do?" He hadn't asked Crystal many questions at the bar. Or after.

She shrugged. "I consult. It's nothing special. Not like you. But it pays the bills, so I gotta get going."

"When can I see you again?"

"That depends."

She walked over to the bed and looked down at him. Her smudged mascara gave the illusion of two black eyes. He reached up and ran a thumb under one eye, and then the other, rubbing the makeup away.

"There, that's better."

She smiled tightly. "You're not married, are you, Red?"

"No, ma'am," he lied.

She studied him for a second. Then she nodded. "Good."

"So, are we gonna get together again?"

He was surprised at how much he wanted to see her again. Usually, he lost interest after he slept with a barfly. But Crystal was different. She was a knockout, good in bed, and a good listener.

"I'll be back tomorrow. Meet at Wingman's?"

"How 'bout I take you out to dinner instead? A proper date."

She leaned over and brushed his lips with hers. "Sure. Let's meet here. Saturday. Five o'clock."

He ran his hands over her bare shoulders. "If we meet here, we might not make it to dinner."

"That's okay, too. See you later, Red."

Another kiss, and she was gone. Out the door before he could take a shot at talking her back into bed. He flopped back on the pillow and replayed the night until he drifted off to sleep for a few more hours of shuteye.

When he woke up, he reached for his phone on the nightstand to check the time and got a handful of nothing. He slapped his palm down on the surface and frowned. He could've sworn he'd tossed it on the bedside table. He flicked on the light. No phone. He hung over the edge of the bed and peered beneath it. Nothing there but dust.

Great. Just great. Must've left it at Wingman's. Whatever. It was just the cheap phone he used to keep his extracurricular activities private from Rebecca. No great loss.

4

Twenty-five miles north, across the Chesapeake Bay, Bodhi King sat on the dewy ground outside his tent, lotus style —cross-legged with his bare feet resting on his thighs—and watched as the purple sky lightened and the first pale orange streak of sun struggled into view above the trees, serenaded by the dawn chorus of wrens, warblers, and thrushes.

The campground was known, not for its sunrises, but for its spectacular sunsets over the water. But Bodhi felt most at home among the songbirds perched in the trees singing their morning song. He rose while the sky was still fully dark and meditated while the birds began their chirping. Then he started a fire and made a mug of tea. He sipped it while the sun's first rays spread across the horizon to shine down on his shoulders.

It was a quiet start to what promised to be a quiet day—his first full day at the campground. He'd planned the trip to coincide with the spring migration, eager to fill his days with birding, hikes, and walks through the woods and along the beach. The solitude, crisp air, and raw beauty of the Eastern Shore would be a balm for his increasingly frantic mind.

Or so he hoped.

He frowned into his mug. At some point in the past few years, his carefully designed life of contemplation and peace had been upended, giving way to busyness and tragedy. Murders, overdoses, espionage. Betrayal, scandals, revenge. This was not his life.

And, yet at some point, it had *become* his life.

He needed to reflect, reset, recalibrate—reconnect with his purpose. That's why he was here. One week in a state park smack in the middle of the Atlantic Flyway. Birds. Trees. Water. Sand. Silence. And, by the end, he hoped he'd find his center once more. Even if it meant losing something else. Or someone else.

He shook his head, dislodging the thought. *The way to enlightenment is non-attachment. Remember this.*

He stood and walked to the bathhouse to rinse out his cup. Then he tucked it into his backpack and turned to face the water. The bay was calling. He skirted around the wooden boardwalk that led down to the beach, preferring to cut his own path through the woods.

As he walked, he focused on each step. His foot pressed against the grass, the rock, the dirt. He felt the sun warming the top of his head. The breeze lifting the straps of his backpack and letting them fall again against his shoulder blades. He inhaled the smell of loam, nuts, and decaying leaves that crinkled and rustled under his sandals. He stopped to watch a squirrel bury an acorn.

When he reached the marsh preserve that led to the beach, he paused for a moment to center himself there in the ancient growth. By the time he reached the sand and unlaced his sandals, his mind was clear and the monkey that had been scrabbling around in his brain was sleeping. He inhaled gratitude. He exhaled peace.

He'd fallen out of the practice of being still the more his life had shifted. In a world that didn't lend itself to contemplation, it was on him to rebuild those muscles and regain his center. He had work to do.

He rested his bag in the sand beside his sandals and strolled along the shoreline. He noted the curves of the shells that the bay had strewn across the beach like fistfuls of glittering jewels. Driftwood rose up like elaborate sculptures, wet from the tide.

A short, plump sandpiper tottered past and dug its bill into the sand to turn over a rock. It plucked out a snail and swallowed it, then turned and studied Bodhi.

"Hi, there." He reached into his pocket and felt around for his handful of cashews.

He crouched and extended his hand, offering a nut to the shorebird. It raced toward him a few steps, then stopped. He waited while the bird tilted its head and gave him a quizzical sideways look with one glassy eye, taking his measure—friend or foe?

"I'm a friend," he assured it.

It turned its head the other way and jutted its neck forward, sussing out whether to believe him.

He stretched his hand out farther, and the bird took quick, but cautious, steps toward him. Ready to bolt if it sensed danger. He squatted, silent and still, until the bird darted forward and plucked the nut from his palm. It ran back a foot or so to nibble it.

Wheet, wheet, wheet.

"You're welcome."

The bird gave him another head tilt, then it sprinted toward him again. They repeated the cashew-run away dance until the bird had its fill. It gave Bodhi a final long look and flew off, beating its wings as it sailed over the bay, just above the surface of the water.

He walked on, then stopped at the edge of the sand to stare out at the Ghost Fleet. Nine World War II-era concrete ships that had been used by the Army in the Pacific Theater. Several years after the war ended, they'd been towed to the Chesapeake Bay, where they were lined up end to end and partially sunk to create a breakwater. Cracked, rusted, and covered with moss and barnacles, the ghost ships were a picture of decay. And yet, they thrummed with life; their decks were crowded with birds—some nesting, some fishing, some squabbling over oysters and other treats.

As he watched, a flurry of heavy wings fluttered and a chorus of agitated squawks rose up from the concrete boats. Large black silhouettes of birds filled the sky above the water. A crow sailed across the bay and landed near Bodhi. The corvid was small, and its glossy black wings shimmered purple in the light. It cawed.

Bodhi patted his pockets. “Hang on. Let me see if I have any more.”

He dug out the last few nuts and proffered them. This bird didn't hesitate, didn't decide. It made a snap decision and bobbed forward with no trepidation to snatch the nuts from his hand.

It ate greedily. When it swallowed the last nut, it took two steps closer to Bodhi and tapped him on the arm. Two sharp pecks with its beak.

The meaning was clear. *More.*

“I think that's it, friend.”

His pockets were empty. The crow objected with a loud shriek. Despite the bird’s displeasure, the insistent sound was different from most crows’ calls —a higher pitch, more nasal, less harsh.

“Okay, okay. I’ll check my bag.”

He headed toward the edge of the preserve where he’d left his sandals and backpack. The crow raced along beside him.

5

Saturday

Red crossed his legs at the ankles and lounged against the trunk of his Mustang, watching the traffic whiz by while he waited for Crystal. He smoothed his shirt over his torso and checked the time again. She'd better not be standing him up. Finally, a gold sedan with Pennsylvania plates turned into the hotel parking lot and slid into the empty spot to his right. He squinted behind his aviator shades, trying to catch a glimpse of her, and hoped she looked as good in the light of day as she had in the beer-infused dimness of Wingman's.

She flashed him a broad smile and gave a little wave as she exited the car.

"Hi, Red. Hope you haven't been waiting too long. I hit traffic." She closed the gap between them with long languid steps.

"Nah," he lied. "Just got here. So, you want to grab a burger? I know a joint on the bay side. Food's just decent, but the view of the sunset is fantastic."

She raised both eyebrows and her gaze drifted to the row of motel room doors over his shoulder. "I pegged you for a dessert first guy."

"I need to eat. Fuel up, you know?"

"Sure, whatever. You want to drive?"

"Yeah. Hop in." He hit the button on the key fob to pop the locks.

She walked to the passenger side and stood beside the door.

"It's unlocked," he told her.

She quirked her lips in a half-smile and folded her arms over her chest. He stared at her for a moment then caught on. He jogged around the car and yanked the door open for her.

"Thanks." She brushed past him and settled herself in the bucket seat.

High maintenance. Not usually what he looked for in a side piece, but her appearance held up in the daylight, so he was inclined to let it slide. For now.

He jumped behind the wheel and started the engine. "Buckle up, buttercup."

He peeled out of the lot and onto the street without bothering to pause at the stop sign. The windows were down, and the wind whipped through their hair.

She whooped with excitement, and he revved the engine and gave the car some gas. The Mustang purred in response.

"You like speed, Crystal?" he called over the noise.

"Yeah. But try not to get pulled over, would you?"

She had a point. His driving record had a few blemishes as it was. He eased off the pedal.

"So, you're a long way from home."

"What?" She eyed him.

"PA plates on your car."

"Oh. Yeah, like I told you, I'm doing some consulting in the area."

Uh oh. Beccs always said he was a terrible listener.

"What kind of consulting?"

"What?" She yelled back, straining to be heard

over the road noise and the rumble of the car.

"Forget it. We'll talk at dinner."

She grinned and settled back into her seat. He drummed a joyful beat on the steering wheel. It was gonna be a great night. He could feel it.

Crystal reached into her purse for Red's cell phone. She pushed it across the wire patio table just as Red took a big gulp of his beer.

"What's this?" he choked out.

"Your phone, isn't it?"

He grabbed it. "What the hell?"

"I must've swept it into my purse by mistake when I left the motel. Didn't you notice it was missing?"

He shoved it in his pocket with a frown. "Sure. I figured I'd left it at Wingman's, but Ace said nobody turned it in. Why didn't you let me know you had it?"

She took a long breath and sipped her cocktail. When she'd swallowed her initial sarcastic response, she smiled. "I couldn't exactly call you, could I? I had your phone, remember?"

He nodded. "I guess."

She waited until his brow relaxed and his shoulders loosened. Then she moved in for the kill. "I mean, I suppose I could've called your main cell phone or your house—but, what if your wife had picked up?"

He sprayed beer all over the table. "What?"

She passed him a fistful of napkins. "Get a hold of yourself, Red. Surely you didn't want me to tell Rebecca I accidentally took your phone after you took me to bed."

"I don't ... what ... how do you ...?" he stammered.

"You think you picked me up at the bar. But the truth is, I chose you. Carefully, I might add. I went to that sticky, dirty bar a half dozen times, looking for just the right man. I watched you work the room, and I knew you were my guy."

That and he had access to the keys she needed, but she'd rather keep the narrative simple until he was on board.

"I didn't notice you."

"You weren't supposed to. I didn't dress to be noticed. I didn't wear makeup or do my hair or sit at the bar."

She'd slouched in a dim corner near the band,

nursing a domestic beer, wearing a ball cap and an oversized sweatshirt. As far as Red was concerned, she might as well have been a plant or one of the cheap prints hanging askew on the walls. But she'd watched three weeks ago as he put the moves on the gin-loving brunette who managed unused properties for the Air Force. Shoot, she'd even put in a good word for him when she arranged to be in the ladies' room at the same time as her. And it had paid off—for her and for Red.

He narrowed his eyes and gripped the neck of the bottle. "So, what is this? Are you a PI? Did Beccs hire you?"

"No, I'm not working for your wife. Calm down."

He laughed bitterly. "I get it. It's a shakedown. How much do you want?"

As he dug into his pocket for his wallet, she sighed and allowed her gaze to drift over his shoulder to the sun dipping into the shimmering water. He was right about the view. She brought her eyes back to his, lowered her chin, and leaned across the table.

"I'm not blackmailing you."

"Then what are you doing?"

"I'm offering you a business opportunity. We'll be partners." She smiled. "With benefits."

6

Red leaned against the railing and pretended to look out over the marsh. But his mind wasn't on the hawk riding a thermal off in the distance, and his casual stance was belied by the uncontrollable jittering of his right leg.

Stay cool, fool.

He sucked in a breath and fought the urge to check his watch again. Crystal said the guy would be here. He'd be here.

Or not.

It occurred to Red that Crystal's contact flaking out was hardly the worst thing that could happen. He still wasn't entirely sure what she—and, by extension, he—was mixed up in. But if this guy ghosted, then maybe Red could extricate himself from this mess before it got any messier. All he'd wanted was a little fun, and somehow he'd ended up enmeshed in what had to be criminal activity.

His part, for sure, was a crime. Giving Crystal's guy access to the bunker was a one-way ticket to the brig if he got caught. His stomach tightened, and he reminded himself that *not* doing it was a one-way ticket to divorce court. If Crystal told Beccs ...

His clenched gut seized, and he grimaced. He dug a roll of antacids out of the pocket of his weathered bomber jacket and popped one in his mouth. He breathed through his nose and tried to ignore his roiling stomach while the chalky tablet got to work.

His mind wandered back to Crystal's parting warning instructions. *"He'll bring his equipment. Open up the bunker and take him to the underground Plotting Room."*

"Then what?" he'd asked.

"Lock him in. Check on him once a day until he finishes his work."

The gunmetal gray glint in her eyes stopped him from asking any questions about what the 'work' entailed or who this guy was. He did ask if he was supposed to feed the man, and she'd shrugged.

"Sure, if you want to. Just don't get too attached."

He decided not to think too hard about what getting attached might mean, and why she didn't want him to. He couldn't believe he'd been dragged into this ... whatever it was.

Drug deal.

It had to be, right? The port in Norfolk was a popular spot for moving product up from Mexico, right under the Navy's nose. Although they insisted that was a Coast Guard issue. Well, whoever's problem it was, now he was about to become part of it.

He didn't have a strong moral objection to that—not really. Beccs wanted to move out of the townhouse. She claimed to feel hemmed in by the constant cacophony of the Johnsons and their six kids packed into the unit to their left and the loud, raucous partying of the ever-changing assortment of college kids who rented the unit to their right. He didn't give a crap about any of the neighbors or their noise, but Beccs was becoming bitter about it.

And Red liked to keep her happy. Despite his extracurriculars, he loved her. A man just needed to burn off energy now and then, as his pop used to say. Didn't mean anything bad about his woman. If he could come up with a chunk of change to put toward a down payment on a single-family house, she'd get off his back.

Viewed this way, he decided, Crystal's little game was less of a problem and more of an opportunity. That was another one of Pop's sayings: Call something a problem, it's a problem. Call it an opportunity, it's an opportunity. It was all a matter of perspective. Of course, his father's last opportunity had earned him a six-to-ten stint as a guest of the Commonwealth.

He kicked at the olive green seabag full of snacks and energy drinks and pushed the negative thoughts out of his head. Just then the hawk swooped down and circled low over the marsh grass, tracking some small prey. He strained to see what was about to become the raptor's lunch when he heard the crunch of tires kicking up gravel. Across the meadow, a taxi circled the lot slowly.

Red waved both arms overhead and then raised his fingers to his mouth and let out a loud, shrill whistle. The cab stopped. He hoisted the bag over his shoulder and jogged down the stairs from the overlook's deck then hoofed it, double time, to the parking lot.

He pulled up short at the edge of the clearing as the cabbie hopped out and opened the rear left door and offered his arm to the man struggling to pull himself out of the back seat. Crystal's expert was rail-thin, pale as paper, and sucking down air at the exertion. Red squinted. He couldn't be any older than his sixties, but he was frail. Delicate, even.

The guy peeled off a couple bills from a brown billfold, the leather worn almost as thin as he was, and pressed them into the cab driver's hand. The driver popped the trunk and pulled out a black suitcase then gestured for Red to come over.

He didn't realize he was also the bellhop. He grumbled colorfully under his breath but crossed the lot and took the heavy case out of the driver's hand like a dutiful host. Up close, he amended his guess: the guy was younger than he looked, maybe mid- to late fifties. But definitely unwell. His skin was gray, his breath rattled, and his eyes were glassy. Maybe he was addicted to his own product.

"Is this it?" he asked.

The driver nodded, slammed the trunk shut, and climbed back into his car. Through the open window, he called a farewell to his passenger. "You take care, now, Mike."

The guy raised a hand and managed a feeble wave as the taxi turned in a slow arc and headed out of the lot. He was still winded from the exertion of getting out of the car. It was going to take them a year and a half to walk back to the bunker, Red realized.

"That your name? Mike?" he asked.

The man gasped and gaped at him, open-mouthed and wide-eyed for a few seconds like a bullfrog. Then he narrowed his eyes and nodded as if he'd solved some sort of mystery. "It is."

His voice was raspy and rough.

"Well, I'm Red. You sound thirsty. After I get you set up, I'll get you something to wet your whistle." He gave the guy a friendly smile.

This guy wasn't in any condition to give Red any trouble, and that was a relief. He'd been picturing a big thug or at least a scrappy dude who had a cloud of violence hanging over him. This guy was a mouse. He must be the chemist, Red decided. The brains, not the brawn, of the outfit.

"Okay, Red." Mike squared his bony shoulders and jutted out his chin. "Lead the way."

7

The young man prattled on like a tour guide as he and Mike made their way through the parking lot, a grassy open area, and past the remnants of an old cemetery. The walk was painstaking and slow. Mike knew the guy was frustrated with their plodding pace, but his aching bones and deteriorating muscles could only carry him so fast.

Just before they reached a paved walk, Red pointed out a brown-shelled tortoise and cracked, "Looks like he wants to race you."

Mike ignored the dig. He'd absorb whatever indignity he had to, do whatever this man wanted, anything to protect his little girl. He gave a dry, rattling laugh and reminded himself that his little girl was twenty-seven. Still, she was his daughter, and it was his duty to keep her safe.

Red grinned broadly, apparently under the misapprehension that Mike was amused at the comparison to the turtle. He was a surprise, Red was. He didn't seem like a violent criminal. And yet, he must be. Mike would have to be careful not to let his guard down and get suckered by the aw, shucks demeanor. He was dealing with dangerous people, and it wouldn't do to forget that.

"So, uh, this is all your equipment?" Red asked, hefting the suitcase.

"I brought what you—or whoever—told me to." It was pretty clear that whatever else he was, Red wasn't the brains of this operation.

As if to prove him right, Red nodded dully. "Okay, then."

He paused in front of a cannon bearing some historical plaque that Mike couldn't quite read from where he stood and gestured to a set of stairs. "Up there, on top of the bunker, there's a deck with an overlook. Good for bird watching and sh—stuff. Uh, but you can check that out some other time."

Mike raised an eyebrow. They both knew that the odds of him making it up those steps were long. Heck, they were nonexistent. He eyed Red, looking for cruelty behind the remark, but the younger guy's face gave no hint of malice. If anything, he seemed amiable. Like a puppy.

"Sure, yeah, later. What is this place?"

"It started out as an Army fort in the 1940s. The Air Force took it over in 1949 and used it for just over thirty years as a station. Now, this whole place is owned by the National Park Service. They allow some nature conservancy group to manage it as a wildlife refuge and preserve."

While Red explained the history, they made their way through a large, cement-walled tunnel. It was cool, dank, and dark. *Like a grave.* The thought popped unbidden into Mike's head. He made no effort to dislodge it. At this point, he was getting himself acclimated to the certainty of death. He figured he might as well.

The abandoned bunker was rusted and discolored. There was a dark, cave-like space hollowed into the right side of the structure with thick steel bars across the opening. Mike stopped walking and stood in front of the cell or cage or whatever it was.

Red walked on a few steps before noticing he'd stopped. He turned and looked over his shoulder. "What are you doing?"

"Isn't this where you're going to hold me?"

"Hold you ... what do you mean, hold you?"

Mike leveled him with a look. He couldn't make out Red's expression in the shadows but the man made no move toward him, so Mike took one last look at the nightmare-inducing cell and shuffled forward. His footsteps echoed off the hard walls.

They continued on in silence until they reached a large steel door cut into the side of the wall. Red dropped the bags to the ground with a thud that sounded like the crack of a gun. Mike winced. He hoped the fragile items in his case had survived the impact. He'd wrapped his pajamas around the tools, but they weren't made to withstand abuse.

Red, unaware that he'd just dropped several hundred thousand dollars' worth of delicate instruments to the ground, scrabbled around in his jacket pocket and pulled out a large keyring. He hummed as he flipped through the keys until he found the one he wanted and shoved it into the keyhole. He turned the key and yanked the door open. The heavy door shrieked in protest as it scraped over the cement.

He held the door open and bowed from the waist like a butler, then waved his hand with a flourish. "After you."

Mike stood, rooted in place, and stared into the dark interior. A musty, metallic odor filled his nostrils, as if the door hadn't been opened in decades.

"Go ahead." Red's clowning around routine vanished, and his voice took on a hard, impatient edge.

Mike swallowed and willed his legs to move. They didn't respond. Red flashed him an angry look.

"I'm ... sorry. I just ... I'm tired from the walk." It was true. He was. But, more than that, he was frozen in terror.

Get it together. Are you going to let them kill her because you couldn't walk into a dark room? You have to get her out of this. Move your ass.

He inched forward, trembling.

Red huffed. He nudged the bags with one foot and kicked them through the doorway—his duffle bag first, and then Mike's case. Then he propped the door open with his side and leaned over to grip Mike's bony arm just above the elbow.

"Come on, then," he piloted Mike through the doorway.

The door slammed closed behind them with a bang and they were plunged into darkness. Mike bit down on his lower lip hard enough to draw blood.

Then Red pulled out a flashlight and aimed it at the door. He engaged the lock then turned to face Mike.

"Come on, the Plotting Room's underground."

"The Plotting Room?"

"Yeah. My girl told me when the Air Force took over, they used it as the NCO club, which seems about right. It's a pit."

"Is there electricity? Light?"

"Yeah. This bulb's burned out, but once we get to the corridor, we'll be able to see. Just hold on to me. I'll get you settled and then come back for the bags."

With no other available options, Mike clung to the man's arm and moved his lips in a silent prayer.

8

Three days later

Devon Currie stifled a sigh as the tent camper from Pennsylvania came into view around the bend. They watched for a moment, hoping the guy had some other destination in mind, but, nope, he was beelining toward the ranger station. They closed their book, straightened the collar on their khaki-colored button-down shirt, and yanked the olive green hat from the shelf at their elbow, jamming it on their head as they mounted the steps.

Devon loved birds. Devon did not love people. In

particular, interacting with people. From a distance, people were fine. This job was a dream job from the bird aspect. The people part was just something they had to awkwardly suffer through in order to live and work in this amazing place. They pasted on a smile and hoped this would be short.

The bell over the door tinkled and the guy loped in, ducking his head under the frame. He cradled a bundle wrapped up in a heather gray t-shirt.

"Morning," Devon greeted him with what little enthusiasm they could muster.

The guy glanced up from whatever he was carrying to meet Devon's gaze with mournful eyes. "I found this bird on the beach."

Not again.

Devon's mouth went dry. They raced around the counter to peer into the swaddled up t-shirt.

"Is it hurt?"

Please let it be hurt. An injured bird, I might be able to help.

But the guy shook his head no, sending his mop of blondish-brown curls bouncing all over. "It's dead. A crow."

Devon's gut twisted as the guy pulled aside the hem of the shirt with a gentle hand to reveal glossy purple-black feathers and an unseeing bead of an eye.

"Fish crow," Devon breathed.

The guy wrinkled his brow. "That's a separate species?"

"Yeah. Very close to the American crow. They can be hard to tell apart. Fish crows have shorter legs, pointier wings, thinner, longer tail. The call is different, too." The words stuck in their throat.

The guy nodded. "I heard it. Not as harsh and deep as the usual caw. Or as loud."

"That's right."

"This guy had a short, high-pitched nasally call." He shifted his gaze to the dead corvid in his arms.

"You mean, this kind of crow."

"No, this crow. I knew him. He was always on the beach just before sunset. Sometimes in the morning, but always in the evening. He liked nuts—hazelnuts most of all."

Devon recognized the birds, and the birds recognized Devon. But most visitors didn't differentiate bird from bird. Even many of the ornithophiles, the hard-core birders, didn't forge relationships with specific birds. There'd been a handful over the years, but they were rare.

"Hazelnuts? That's Captain. He's one of a

handful of the crow who brings—brought—me little gifts." They gestured to the window ledge covered with scraps of metal, shiny rocks, glittering foil gum wrappers, and assorted tokens.

"I'm sorry. I can tell you loved him."

Devon's eyes snapped up. But there was no mockery in this guy's expression—only kindness and sadness.

"Thanks." They reached out a hand to stroke Captain's crown.

"Don't."

Devon pulled their hand back and blinked.

"I mean, I wouldn't," the guy said in a softer voice. "He may have a contagious disease."

The camper gave voice to Devon's worst fear, the terror that woke them night after night. "How do you know? Are you a veterinarian?"

"No. But I do have medical training, and we know avian-to-human transmission is possible."

Devon shoved their hands in their pockets. "Sure, right. But if a virus is killing them, I'm pretty sure it hasn't jumped species."

"Them?"

Devon bit down on their lip, thinking, and studied the guy. Nobody else seemed interested in their theories, but this man had taken the time to bring Captain's body to the station. He'd taken the time to get to know Captain. After a long moment, he gulped and blurted the words.

"Can I show you something?"

Bodhi trailed the ranger—Devon, according to the name tag crookedly affixed to the olive green uniform shirt—through the door leading to the back of the office/campground store. He still held the t-shirt-wrapped dead crow in his arms.

They walked through a short hallway and entered a storeroom. The ranger flipped on a light, and a bulb flickered to life overhead. A long chest freezer sat against the far wall next to a clear refrigerator case—the type you'd find stocked with wine in a fancy kitchen, although this one held Styrofoam cups full of live bait.

Devon lifted the lid on the freezer and swept an arm dramatically over the contents. "Look."

Bodhi crossed the room and peered inside. A row of stiff, dead birds stared up at him with sightless eyes. He did a quick count. Five birds—a gull, two egrets, a heron, and a crow. *Two crows*, he corrected himself, as he gently placed Captain next to the other crow.

"What is this?"

"I was hoping you could tell me. All these birds have died within the last three days." The ranger's voice was tight and vibrated with emotion.

Bodhi shook his head. "I'm sorry. I don't have any expertise in this area."

"You said you have medical training." Devon's tone was accusatory.

"I do. Well, I'm a doctor, but I specialize in forensic pathology. I'm a pathologist." He saw the spark of hope in the ranger's eyes and hurriedly specified, "A *human* pathologist."

Devon waved away the clarification. "That's even better than being a vet. Your job is to find out the cause of death, right?"

"In people."

"Dead is dead," the ranger insisted.

Bodhi shrugged. It was true. And he, of all people, knew the value of a life—any life, be it an ant, a man, or a fish crow. He stared down at the row of cold bodies lined up in the freezer, struck by the eerie similarity between Devon's makeshift body storage system and the metal morgue freezer drawers that slid out from the wall. The ranger had even attached neatly lettered bands to the birds' feet, like so many miniature toe tags.

"I can try," he finally said. "So long as you understand this isn't in my wheelhouse."

"Doesn't matter. At least you give two craps."

He jerked his head up at the bitterness in the ranger's voice. "Did you report this up your chain of command?" he asked slowly, already knowing what the answer would be.

"Of course. They sent out an environmental specialist to test the water and the sand."

"And?"

A stiff-shouldered shrug. Then, "There's no environmental reason for the mass die-off. That's what they're calling it. Usually, the culprit is an algae bloom—toxins or bacteria in the water—when something like this happens. But this is a big birding area. We're a major stopover on the Atlantic Flyway. We're really careful."

He thought for a moment. "Could it be pesticide drift? A nearby farmer spraying a harmful herbicide?" He'd encountered that once before on a case in a farming town in the Midwest.

"Sure, it *could* be. But this is the Chesapeake Bay Area. The locals are pretty proud of it—and protective. I can't imagine any of our neighbors being that careless. And our closest neighbor is an actual wildlife refuge and preserve. Not a chance it came from them. No, something—or *someone*—else is killing these birds." Devon met Bodhi's eyes. "Do you really think you can find out what?"

"Or who."

"Or who."

Bodhi thought. It wouldn't be so different from consulting on any other puzzling case. Inspect the dead. Inspect the last know location. Gather all the disparate pieces and fit them together in a life or death jigsaw puzzle. He could help this ranger protect the rest of the birds. "I think I can."

The ranger managed a tremulous smile. "I can't pay you. I mean, I can ask my supervisor but—"

"Please, don't worry about it. Consider it my tribute to Captain and his fellow birds. Can you think of anything at all that these birds have in common?"

"Sorry, I can't. I've been racking my brain over it for days. They have different diets, different habits. Other than the fact that they're all here, and they're all dead, there's nothing to tie them together."

Bodhi knew that was wrong. *Something* connected these birds. He leaned over the freezer and studied the dead avians more closely. Then he dug a pair of blue medical gloves out of his backpack and snapped them on. He reached into freezer and turned the snowy egret's head to the side.

"Look, do you see this green stain on the neck?" He pointed to a faint spot high on the side of the egret's slender white neck, just below the beak.

Devon bent forward and squinted at the spot. "Yeah? What is it?"

"I think it's biliverdin."

"What's that?"

"It's green bile. It's what sometimes gives a bruise a greenish tinge."

"Okay? What's it mean?"

"Well, biliverdin is the precursor to bilirubin. They both occur during the breakdown of red blood cells. You've heard of jaundice, right?"

"Yeah, little kids get it. They turn yellow."

It was close enough for a layperson. "Right. That yellow cast is caused by bilirubin—yellow bile. And jaundice is a symptom of acute lead poisoning in young children. If birds produce biliverdin rather than bilirubin, then it's possible that green staining would be a symptom of acute lead poisoning in birds."

He turned each of the birds' bodies, one by one, looking for the telltale green. The crows were too dark for it to show if it was present, but he spotted a patch of green on the light gray feathers of the little gull.

"So, what's the next step?"

"If I had access to a lab, I'd autopsy one of the birds, looking for biliverdin discoloration in the gullet and the liver."

Devon blanched.

"Don't worry. I don't have the equipment or materials I need. So, we'll do this the old-fashioned way."

"And what's that?"

"A fishing expedition. Cast a line, and see what bites."

The image of the groups of fishing enthusiasts who crowded the wooden pier and kayaked out to the concrete fleet flashed in his mind. *Cast a line, and see what bites.* A theory was taking shape in his mind. He turned to the ranger.

"Could I borrow a kayak?"

"Sure, but ... why?"

"Call it a hunch."

9

Wednesday morning
Just after sunrise

Bodhi woke shivering in his sleeping roll and inhaled deeply, filling his lungs with the cold, misty air. Sleeping outside was a more effective morning jumpstart than a cup of the strongest coffee—though he knew a few people who'd beg to differ. He raised his arms overhead in a stretch, then unzipped the insulated roll, and pulled a sweatshirt over his head.

After sun salutations, a sitting meditation, and a

mug of tisane, he was ready. He picked up his phone to slip it into his pocket, then reconsidered. Who would he possibly call from a kayak? And as far as he knew, the device wasn't waterproof. He placed it on his pillow and then stepped out of the tent, zipping the mosquito netting up behind him.

Devon had said the kayak would be waiting for him at the kayak launch. He cut through the amphitheater to get to the wooden deck and boardwalk. He only made it as far as the cluster of rental homes that lined the overlook. There, at the edge of the path, lay a stiff-legged loon, its mouth hanging open, its neck bent at an unnatural angle.

He knew before he bent to examine it. *Dead.* He cupped his hands around the bird's small head and raised his eyes to the weak, still-rising sun. His memory of the appropriate sutta was rusty—which, given his line of work, was frankly inexcusable. So he came as close as he could, intoning, "Like this bird, I will one day be. I share a nature with its body. I am not exempt from death. I should do good with my body, mind, and words." His mind returned to his days in Pittsburgh, working with Saul, and their familiar refrain: "The cause of death is life."

And yet. He couldn't shake the feeling that the

loon's life had been cut short by an unseen hand. Wishing the bird good karma, he placed it out of the footpath, where Devon would be sure to see it, before he continued on his way to the beach.

The stairs were rickety, and the wind was strong, so by the time he reached the so-called solid ground, Bodhi was grateful for it—even if it was made up of shifting sand. He untied the kayak and pocketed the hand-drawn sign that proclaimed "Reserved for Dr. B. King." He was carrying the craft to the launch, when he spotted yet another bird.

A goose, on its back, feet splayed and pointing up in the air. *Definitely dead,* he thought, making the determination from a distance. He drew closer anyway. As he walked over to it, he considered the impermanence of life and the certainty of death. He looked down at the creature. Who was he to say his life was greater or more valuable than this bird's?

Spurred by the two most recent bird deaths, he moved with urgency. He grabbed the life vest from the cockpit, shrugged into it, and clipped it closed. He set the kayak at the edge of the water, settled into the seat, and pushed off the sand with his paddle. The boat glided into the estuary, and he began to paddle, making short, smooth strokes through the glassy water. He breathed in the salty air and aimed the craft toward the concrete ships that loomed offshore.

The short distance, the calm waters, and a sense of purpose propelled him to the line of ships in just a few minutes. He lined up with the channel between two of the ships and floated through it, then reversed his paddling to bring the kayak to a stop. A handful of anglers bobbed in the shadow of the fleet, fishing from their kayaks. In the distance, a bottle-nosed dolphin splashed up to greet the sun.

"Morning," said the woman fishing from the nearest kayak.

"Good morning."

She watched him from beneath her tan fishing hat as he paddled over to the side of a ship with a chunk of exposed rebar and tied the kayak to the steel rods.

He was checking his knots when she called to him, "We're not supposed to fish from those ships."

He gave the rope a final tug, then nodded. "I'm not fishing. I'm a consultant working with one of the park rangers."

She gave him a cool look but said nothing. Instead she turned back to her lines, and he clambered up the crumbling concrete hull. When he reached the deck, a chorus of irritated birds squawked at him. Several took flight with an agitated flap of wings. He circled the ship's wide deck taking slow, cautious steps—both to minimize the disruption to the birds and to test the structural soundness of the decaying ship.

The ship was a mess. Or it was a thriving ecosystem, depending on one's point of view. The birds had claimed it as their own, as evidenced by the nests, perches, and piles of fish guts littering the space. As he circled the wide expanse of concrete, a curious crow scampered along behind him. He paused to dig some dried fruit out of his bag. The bird took the offered treat without hesitation.

Bird waste covered the deck. Bodhi bent to inspect a splotch. It was green. His eyes scanned the deck. Green smears dotted the deck. More biliverdin, more evidence of lead poisoning. The bird at Bodhi's heels cawed.

"What's up, buddy?"

It cocked its head at the sound of his voice, then raced off to the far corner of the ship, nudging a heron out of its way. Bodhi resumed his study of the bird poop. He was certain that if he had the means to test a sample, he'd find elevated lead levels. He rocked back on his heels to think it through.

Assuming he'd identified the *why*, the next—and most pressing—question to answer was *how*. How were the birds ingesting toxic amounts of lead? Lead could be accumulating in the fish, but some of the affected birds weren't fish eaters. And, besides, the Chesapeake Bay Watershed was protected waters. It was unlikely that there was lead runoff entering the bay. So, where was the lead coming from?

His musings were interrupted by the return of the crow, who dropped two metal items at his feet with a dull thunk and sat down beside the offerings. Bodhi examined the presents: a metal fishing weight and an object shaped like a two-prong plug. He picked up the glittery fishing weight and considered it for a moment before turning his attention to the plug thingie. It was a small rectangular case with two shiny metal pins protruding from the bottom and a notch cut into the top. The black-painted face was engraved with the words "Crystal Holder" and "U.S. Army Signal Corp." A series of numbers identified a frequency and an order number. "Alfred Hartman Mfg. Co. Carlisle, PA" was etched on the side, and the top frequency number was repeated on the notched handle. It was weathered and scratched, but it retained enough shine that he understood why the crow had gifted it to him. He pocketed it and returned his attention to the fishing tackle, bouncing it in his palm to get a sense of its weight.

"Did you just give me my *how,* friend?"

The crow cawed in response.

10

Mike was bent over the grinder. When he heard the metallic echo of the door slamming closed outside the Plotting Room he wiped the sweat from his brow and turned off the machine. As he was removing his dust mask, Red entered the room clutching a grease-stained white takeout bag.

"Lunch."

Mike inhaled. "Let me guess, burgers?"

"And fries." Red placed the bag on the counter just inside the door and removed a bottle of root beer from his jacket pocket. "And a soda."

"Thanks."

The younger guy shoved his hands in his pockets. "Sure. So ... uh, how's it going?"

"Come and take a look."

Red crossed the room and peered over Mike's shoulder. "I don't know what I'm looking at."

"I'm in the first stage of grinding the blanks."

"Still?"

Mike shrugged. "I know it's slow going. I'm sorry, kid. I just don't have the stamina to work this equipment for very long."

Red flushed, and Mike knew he was remembering how he'd damaged the tools in Mike's case. The truth was, the broken tools were only useful for the final precision stage of grinding, but Red didn't seem to understand this.

"I ..."

"Luckily all this grinding equipment is still operational," Mike hurried to reassure him.

"And you're *sure* you can do everything you need to do with this dusty old stuff?" He waved a hand dismissively at the ancient lapping machine.

He had no idea, Mike realized. This dusty old stuff had been state of the art—a marvel of technological innovation—when the wartime manufacturing complex had cranked it out in the early 1940s. Not that Mike was around then himself, but he'd grown up on a steady diet of his grandfather's stories.

"Definitely."

"And what exactly are you doing anyway?"

Mike raised his eyebrows. He'd been at it now for four days, and this was the first interest Red had shown.

"Well, that box you gave me the first night contained slabs of rough-cut galena crystals. I cut them into slices and identified their polarity. You know what that is?"

"Negative and positive charge, sure."

"Right. After I determined their polarity, I mounted them on this jig to sawcut them into thin discs. That's what I'm in the middle of now."

"This galena stuff, it's valuable? Like gemstones?"

Mike snorted and slapped his thigh. The laughter set off a bout of coughing and choking. He gasped and scrabbled around on the table for his inhaler. *Puff. Puff. Breathe. Breathe.*

Red watched him, worry contorting his face. After a long moment, Mike rasped, "I guess it's valuable enough to some people. Otherwise, you and I wouldn't be here, would we. And my kid's life wouldn't be in danger."

"Your kid?"

He cut his eyes sharply toward the younger man. Red's brow was furrowed and his eyes were screwed up like he was concentrating hard. He gave no indication he knew what Mike was talking about. If it was an act it was a good one.

"Yeah. They've got my daughter. They said if I ever want to see her alive again, I'll do what you say. You really didn't know?"

Red gaped at him, his eyes huge. A mottled pink stain crept up his neck. Without warning, he turned and sprinted out the door. Mike heard his feet clang against the metal stairs and then pound against the ground overhead.

As soon as the sound faded, he pulled the dust mask back over his nose and mouth and turned the grinder back on. He had work to do. The image that he'd seen when he opened the text from an unknown number last Saturday morning—his daughter, gagged and bound, her eyes wide and pleading—was burned into his mind. He saw it even when he slept. He choked and coughed, a nasty rattling sound, but kept his head bent over the grinder and focused on steadying his trembling hands. He couldn't afford to stop.

Red raced up the stairs and out of the bunker, his heart thundering, and fumbled for the phone. He punched in the number that Crystal had given him and was shouting before she finished saying hello.

"You kidnapped Mike's daughter?" he roared.

"Take it easy."

"Answer the question."

"I will. Once you calm down."

Her patient, soothing tone grated, and he squeezed the cellphone, on the verge of exploding. "Crystal, I want an answer. Did you—or whoever you're working with—grab this guy's daughter? Yes or no?"

There was a long pause. Red paced in front of the historical marker that explained the bunker's history and listened to his heart thump against his rib cage.

Finally, she said, "One, the only person I'm working with is you. It's just you and me, Red. And, two, I haven't kidnapped anybody, okay?"

He exhaled and tried to steady his breath. "Okay. Good."

"You need to focus on keeping him on task

instead of his listening to his ramblings. What's taking so long, anyway?"

It was Red's turn to fall silent. He hadn't yet told her about dropping Mike's equipment and breaking it.

"Red? I know how long it takes grind those blanks."

"There's a problem with his equipment. It got ... damaged."

"So? The whole point of doing this in the bunker is that there's a freaking room full of crystal grinding machines and supplies. He knows how to use that ancient stuff—don't let him tell you otherwise." Her briefly conciliatory tone sharpened.

"Yeah, he's using the old machines. He can only work for like an hour or two at time, then he starts coughing and gasping. He can't breathe. He gets worn out and has to rest. I think he's really sick. It seems—"

"Boo hoo. I don't want to hear it. Do what you have to, but keep him working."

Red sucked on his teeth and thought. "What do you have on him? If you didn't snatch his daughter, why is he here? Why's he doing this?"

On the other end of the phone, Crystal sighed

heavily. "I'm going to level with you. Just stay cool, would you?"

His stomach clenched. He didn't like where this was going. "Yeah, okay. Just spit it out."

"His daughter is fine. But he *thinks* she's being held captive until he produces functional galena radio crystals."

"What? Why?"

"Because we're going to sell them on the black market. That's why."

"To who?"

"To *whom*. And don't worry about it. I've got the buyer all lined up. All you need to do is motivate our friend."

A sour taste rose in his throat. "This is wrong."

It was wrong. It was cruel to mess with Mike this way. And Red wasn't even sure he could trust her. What if she was lying, what if Mike's daughter really had been abducted? He wanted no parts of this. A little quick money and some fun with a hottie, that was one thing. This was something else entirely.

Crystal barked out a brittle laugh. "Were you under the impression that this was all sunshine, lollipops, and rainbows, Red? Just do what I say."

"Or what?"

"Do you really need to ask?"

Of course he didn't. She'd tell Beccs about them. She had him by the short hairs, and they both knew it.

"She'll forgive me," he blustered with more confidence than he felt.

"You think so? Maybe she'd forgive one indiscretion. But it's not just me. What about Kathleen, the brunette in charge of the surplus properties? Or that bubbly blonde waitress at Wingman's? What's her name? Oh, right, Melody. Shall I go on?"

"How do you ...?" He trailed off and stared at the phone in his hand. That's how. She went through his phone.

As if she was reading his mind, she said, "I cloned it, by the way. Not just the texts. I have a copy of your camera reel too. So I suggest you stop worrying about Mike's health and focus on his productivity."

She hung up without waiting for a response.

11

After Bodhi kayaked back to the park, he went in search of Devon. But the door to the ranger's office was locked. He wandered back to the beach and hung around the fishing pier hoping to make eye contact with someone in a talkative mood.

But everyone seemed to be keeping their attention fully on the fish. He was just about to tap an older gentleman on the shoulder and ask how the fish were biting, when he spotted the kayak angler whom he'd met out at the ghost ship coming ashore with her friends. He hurried down to the beach and approached them as they were getting out of their boats.

"Excuse me?"

"Yeah?" She grabbed the end of the dock and pulled herself up out of the kayak.

"Do you know what kind of weight this is?" He held out the fishing knoch that the crow had given him.

She exchanged a look with one of her fellow anglers—a bald guy with a wide forehead and a gold hoop earring—before answering. "It's a lead barrel sinker. Decent for catching striped bass, I suppose."

"Eels are better," her friend interjected.

"Well, yeah."

"But it's lead? You're sure."

Her cheek twitched as she suppressed her reaction and shrugged instead. "I'm not sure, but that's what it looks like."

"We don't use any lead tackle, man," the guy with the earring insisted.

"You don't?"

The woman shook her head. "We really don't. It's a hot-button issue around here because of the Atlantic Flyway. Lead tackle is a known danger to waterfowl and raptors."

"Why?"

"They eat it."

"Dumbasses," her friend grumbled.

Bodhi sensed he wasn't talking about the birds.

"Hal," she warned.

"They are."

She waved a hand, "Ignore him. Anyway, we met with the people from the avian conservancy group and voluntarily agreed not to use it. In return, they agreed not to push for a ban."

"But that doesn't stop the tourists," Hal insisted.

"So there are people fishing here who use lead sinkers and weights? Would you say there are a lot?"

"Not really. We host a cleanup with the bird advocates. Once a month, we all come out and clear discarded tackle and other trash from the marsh and the shoreline. Some folks who are into scuba diving even bring their gear and comb the floor. There's not tons of lead, but we pick up all that we can find."

"And this is all an effort to prevent bird deaths—it's not a response to a spate of deaths?"

"Ah, hell," Hal said sourly. "I knew it."

"Pardon?" Bodhi turned to the man.

"Obviously you know a bunch of birds have died this week. We've seen 'em, too. Some of them were stumbling around off-balance, like a bunch of drunks, before they died. Ah, don't tell me—are you from the EPA?"

Bodhi held up his palm. "Let me stop you right there. I don't work for the government. I'm just curious about all the dead birds. I found this sinker and I wondered."

"It's probably those conservancy freaks, trying to frame us."

"Nobody's trying to frame us," the woman argued.

"You don't know that, April."

She scoffed.

"You *don't.*"

"Okay, Hal. Whatever you say."

Bodhi didn't think Hal's theory was as out there as April seemed to believe, but he kept his opinion to himself. He dropped the lead sinker into his pocket, and his hand brushed against the crystal holder. He removed it and held it up.

"I don't suppose either one of you know what this is?"

April leaned in to examine it, then shook her head,

"No. Hal?"

He put his tackle box down in the sand and walked closer.

"Let me see." He held out his hand, and Bodhi deposited the object into his palm.

Hal squinted at the little box. "Well, it was before my time, but the Army used those during World War

II for communications. There's an exhibit about it over at the old fort."

"Fort?" Bodhi asked.

"Sure," Hal explained, pointing across the bay. "See that fire tower jutting out from the trees?"

"Yeah."

"You could paddle right over there. It only takes about fifteen minutes. It used to be an Air Force station, and before that, it was an Army fort. But now it's a nature preserve. The military portions have been abandoned, but there's still a display at the old visitors' center. And there are some historical markers and plaques throughout the park. I know in the displays that I've seen pictures that look that this thing here." Hal handed back the crystal holder.

April chimed in, "And the wildlife conservancy has some displays there, too, and pamphlets about the lead tackle issue and the local wildlife and ecosystem. You could kill two birds with one stone."

Bodhi grimaced at her choice of words.

"Sorry," she said, giving him a sheepish smile.

"It's okay. Thanks for the help."

He slipped the crystal holder into his backpack and headed across the beach to retrieve the kayak.

Crystal sat on the edge of the bed and gnawed on a hangnail. The call with Red pressed down on her shoulders like a weight. She couldn't risk screwing up the sale. These people were dangerous. If the buyer thought she wasn't going to deliver .... She shivered. She didn't want to think about it.

Avoidance isn't going to solve anything, she told herself firmly.

She raised her head and squared her shoulders. Then she leaned forward to grip the edge of the motel dresser and stare at her reflection, saying the words aloud to herself. "If you don't come through with the goods, they're going to find your body floating in the Chesapeake."

She studied herself while that reality sunk in. It was true. And it was all the motivation she needed to stay focused and keep Red focused, too. Keep him in line and on task.

A slow smile spread across her lips.

"I can do that," she said to the empty hotel room.

She knew how to control Reid Serrano. She'd start with the carrot. She leaned into the mirror to fluff her hair and caught a glimpse of her ragged cuticles. Step one would be some maintenance and upkeep. Head to the mall. Get a manicure, maybe a pedicure, too. Hit the boutique and get some lingerie. Then swing by the makeup counter for a new lipstick. A quick stop at the grocery store for some booze. Spend some time slathering Red with attention, and by morning, he'd be back in line.

She exhaled, relief and belief in her plan coursing through her and easing her tension. She snatched up her keys and her purse. As she locked the door behind her and crossed the parking lot, she nodded to herself. If the carrot didn't work, she always had her stick. She hadn't been bluffing. In the closet, locked inside the chintzy motel safe that sat next to the flimsy ironing board, was the copy she'd cloned of Mike's phone. If she couldn't control him the easy way, she had her insurance policy.

But when she jammed the key into the ignition and started the car, Red's worried voice echoed in her mind: *He can't breathe. He gets worn out and has to rest. I think he's really sick.*

What if it's true? What if he is sick, so sick that he couldn't finish the crystals? Then what would she do? What if he's dying?

The questions clawed at her. Guilt tried to bubble up. She pushed it down. It rose again. She jabbed a finger at the button to turn on the radio.

Ugh. A trite, overplayed song blared from the speakers. But she cranked the volume, turning it up to drown out the thoughts that tried to crowd into her mind.

Too bad if he was sick. He'd have to find a way to work through it. Sacrifice came second nature to him, anyway.

And if he died? It served him right.

She buzzed down the windows and sang along to the stupid song.

12

Bodhi tied up the kayak and made his way from the shore to the path that wound through a meadow and an old private cemetery. Along the way, he stopped to read the Plexiglas displays that described the species that lived in the preserve and the conservatory's efforts to protect them. A separate set of markers that lined the path to the overlook identified some of the migratory birds visitors most commonly spotted.

He plucked a pamphlet titled "What You Need To Know About Lead Poisoning in Birds" from a holder affixed to the side of a display about raptors and skimmed it. It largely repeated what April and Hal had told him and confirmed his belief that the dead birds were suffering from lead poisoning. He folded the sheet into thirds and stuffed it into his backpack before continuing on.

When he reached the gravel parking lot that separated the trails from an old military base, he circled the lot. In front of the covered entrance to the visitors' center, he spotted the exhibit Hal had mentioned. A large Plexiglas case displayed several black-and-white photographs and a short article discussing the U.S. Signal Corps and the use of crystal radios to send and receive reliable transmissions in the field during World War II. One of the photographs showed an open case shaped like a long metal toolbox. Padding of some sort was affixed to the lid. Inside, approximately sixty holders like one in his bag were lined up in three neat rows, each with a different number etched on its handle. Several closeup photographs of individual crystal holders left no doubt that they were nearly identical to the one the crow had placed at his feet on the concrete ship. But he dug it out of the bag and compared it to the photograph anyway.

The one he was holding had slightly thicker pins and a blockier top handle, and the crystal holders in the photograph bore the name of a different manufacturer. But it was clear that the object he'd found had been part of a set like the one in the picture. According to the sign, after the war, the U.S. Signal Corps brought back one of the dozens of mobile crystal grinding repair units that had operated in Australia, the Pacific, and Europe. It was currently in storage in the bunker. A historical society was raising funds to establish a crystal radio museum that would preserve the history and science behind the wartime crystal grinders.

He turned the worn holder over and over in his hand, considering it. There was little doubt the box had come from here. But, after seventy-five years, why were these materials turning up miles away on the ghost fleet? Was someone dumping them or had a bird gotten inside the bunker to scavenge for treasure?

He tried the door to the visitors' center. Locked. He shielded his eyes with his hands and pressed his face up to the glass but saw no movement in the dim interior. He circled the concrete battery, seeing no evidence of birds or trash, then climbed the stairs to the overlook on top. He gazed out at the marsh and watched a hawk circle overhead, a dark shape against the clear cerulean sky.

A sharp metallic bang sounded from below and echoed off the expanses of concrete. He wheeled around and leaned over the railing in time to see a man with military-short cropped hair emptying a wastebasket into a dumpster he hadn't seen on his survey of the area. Tucked behind a tall fence, the trash receptacle was visible from above, but not from the ground. A janitor was exactly who he needed to talk to. He swiped his bag off the bench and raced down the stairs two at a time as he slung the straps over his shoulders.

"Hey, hey, excuse me!" he called as he ran across the pavement.

The guy turned around, glaring. "What?"

Bodhi stopped about six feet away, disinclined to draw closer. The man spoke harshly and stood with his legs planted and his hands fisted by his sides, neck tendons straining. *Bellicose, belligerent, brash.* The words flashed through Bodhi's mind in warning.

"Do you work here?"

"No." He was already turning away, in no mood to chat.

Bodhi called after him, "I was up on the overlook bird-watching."

He eyed Bodhi over his shoulder. "Yeah? Well, find another place to watch them. This overlook's closed."

"I didn't see a sign."

"Well, I just told you. So now you know."

Bodhi waited a beat and then walked past the man toward the fence that concealed the dumpster, digging into his back pocket for the pamphlet.

"Hey, I told you to get lost."

"Just have to toss something in the recycling," Bodhi said, raising his hands in a gesture of appeasement and waving the flyer. He stepped behind the fence and opened the dumpster.

The man was right behind him. "There's no recycling back here. You need to move along."

"I thought you didn't work here?" Bodhi's tone was mild, but he didn't turn around. Instead, he peered into the open trash.

"Look, man. Beat it." The guy grabbed him by the shoulders and spun him around. "Why are you so interested in the trash?"

Unwilling to lie, Bodhi told him the truth. "I'm camping at the state park. There's been a rash of dead birds over there. It looks like they've ingested toxic levels of lead, and I'm just trying to figure out where they're getting into that much lead. That's all."

"What are you, some kind of veterinarian?"

"No. I *am* a doctor, though. I offered to look into it because I specialize—"

"Wait, you're a doctor? Like, for people?"

Something that looked a lot like hope washed over the man's face, blotting out the anger and suspicion.

"I am, but—"

Before he could explain that he didn't treat live people, the guy gripped him by the arm and pulled him back across the lot toward the bunker. "I need your help."

13

The man hustled Bodhi through a long, dank cement hallway. The only sound was their footsteps striking the ground and echoing off the walls. When they reached a large metal door, the guy came to a stop and released Bodhi's arm to dig a keyring out of his jacket pocket.

As he jangled the keys, searching for the one to open the door, Bodhi cleared his throat.

"I'm Bodhi King, by the way."

The guy stuck a key in the door and turned to blink at Bodhi. "Oh, sorry. Reid. Reid Serrano. Everybody calls me Red, though."

He rested the trash can on the ground and pumped Bodhi's outstretched hand.

"Serrano—like the pepper?"

"Yeah. Hence the nickname."

"Pleased to meet you."

"Oh, you have no idea how glad am I to meet you, Dr. King."

"Please, call me Bodhi."

Red's eyes narrowed. "But you *are* a doctor, right?"

"I am, but—"

"—Good. Mike needs a doctor."

Red pushed the door open and went inside. Bodhi followed him into a dark hallway and the heavy door closed behind him with a clang. Red reached up and batted at a metal chain until he made contact and yanked down on it. A bare bulb illuminated the space. There wasn't much to see. More cement, mainly.

"Come on, we're going down these stairs." Red pointed to a steep stairwell.

"What's down there?"

"That's where we're working," Red explained as they clomped down the stairs. "In the Plotting Room."

The Plotting Room?

"What's that?"

"When this was a bunker during World War II, the Army used this room as a control center to coordinate the defense. After the Air Force took it over, it was the noncommissioned officers' club.

"And now?"

"Now it's nothing, at least not officially. The Air Force hasn't used it since the 1980s."

Bodhi studied Red in the dim light. His haircut, bearing, and speech patterns all screamed 'military.'

"Are you in the Air Force, Red?"

"No, sir. I do fly, though. I'm a fighter pilot with the Navy. Stationed over in Norfolk."

Red clamped his mouth shut in a hurry, as if he'd said too much. Bodhi pretended not to notice. They reached the bottom of the metal staircase and Red made a quick right turn that led to another metal door. He pushed it open and ushered Bodhi inside.

The smell of must and hot metal tickled Bodhi's nose and the shriek of machinery filled the air. On the far side of the room, an older man—Mike, presumably—was bent over a large piece of equipment.

"Mike," Red shouted to be heard over the squealing metal. "Mike!"

The man turned. His eyes, magnified by

prescription goggles, went wide. He killed the machine, pushed up the safety glasses and removed his dust mask.

"Who's this?"

"I was taking the trash out." Red waved the trashcan in the air as a visual aid before depositing it just along the wall with a resounding bang. "I ran into this guy."

"You don't know him?"

"No."

Mike's eyes flitted from Red's face to Bodhi's and then back. "You think that's smart, bringing someone around?"

Bodhi noted the mild tone Mike used—as if he didn't want to second-guess Red—and wondered about the power dynamic between the two men. Before Red could answer, a fit of coughing wracked Mike's body. He shook in his chair, his chest heaving. He wheezed. His breath crackled and whistled as he struggled to inhale and exhale.

Red looked at Bodhi. "See?"

Bodhi crossed the room and knelt beside Mike's chair. He could hear the rattle of his breath. Sputum dotted his bluish lips. His skin was paper-thin and translucent, revealing the network of blue-green veins running under the surface.

"Do you have a bronchodilator?"

Mike nodded, clawing at the table.

Bodhi stood, pushed aside a cloth, and unearthed the inhaler. He shook it vigorously and removed the cap. "Ready?"

Mike nodded, and Bodhi pointed the canister upward and lined the mouthpiece up with Mike's mouth. He clamped his lips around the inhaler.

As Mike inhaled a fast breath, Bodhi pressed the button and counted aloud. "One. Two. Three. Four. Five."

Then Mike opened his mouth and exhaled slowly.

"Two puffs?"

Mike shook his head no and held up one finger. Bodhi recapped the inhaler and glanced at the prescription label. Mike was taking a combination corticosteroid and a beta agonist. Bodhi found a bottle of water on the shelf above the worktable and held it up to the man's lips.

"Rinse."

Mike took a sip of water, swished it around in his mouth, and spat it on the floor. Bodhi studied his face. He looked spent, shaky, and very tired. The blue tinge around his lips was pronounced.

"May I see your hands?"

Mike held out his hands, palms down. They shook. Bodhi held his wrists and gently turned his palms face up. The skin on his fingertips was wrinkled, loose, and a dark purplish-blue.

"What is it, Doc—Bodhi?" Red asked, still standing in the doorway as if he were glued to the floor.

"Your friend is cyanotic. There's not enough oxygen in his blood."

Bodhi crouched and peered up into Mike's face. "You're dying, Mike."

Mike closed his eyes and nodded.

"Silicosis?"

Another nod. Bodhi frowned at the fine dust particles that covered the workspace. Even with the liquid that had been running while the machine ran, even with the dust mask, working with quartz at this late stage of the disease was suicidal. He narrowed his eyes. The dust was black, not white.

"This isn't quartz?"

Mike's eyelids fluttered. "No. Galena."

"I'm not familiar ..."

"Also known as lead glance. It's another crystallized mineral, like quartz." His voice was raspy, breathy, and slow.

Lead glance. Bodhi's pulse ratcheted up, but he pushed the thought away. *Not now.*

"Okay. Red and I are going to help you to his car." He paused and uttered a silent prayer that Red had a vehicle on-site.

Mike's eyelids pulsed again. "Why?"

"We're going to the hospital."

"No!"

"No!"

Mike and Red's objections overlapped. Bodhi focused on the man in front of him.

"Mike, why?"

His eyes opened, and he fixed Bodhi with a watery gaze. "You said it yourself. I'm dying. I have to get this done while I still can."

"Get what done?"

But the man's head lolled back against the headrest of his chair and his eyes shut.

Bodhi studied his face for a moment and then crossed the room to talk to Red.

"Can you help him?" Red asked.

"No. He needs supplemental oxygen, at a minimum. He needs to go to the hospital."

Red swallowed audibly. "That's not an option."

Bodhi looked at Red for a long moment. The man squirmed under the weight of his gaze at first, then pressed his mouth into a firm, flat line and narrowed his eyes.

Bodhi didn't sugarcoat the news.

"The only other option is death. A lingering, painful one."

Red blanched, but his expression didn't change.

14

Red blinked at Bodhi King. His brain buzzed, thoughts racing. He was in over his head. He'd suspected that for a while now, but the truth of it hit him in the gut.

The doctor insisted that Mike needed medical care. And, really, it didn't take an expert to see that. He'd looked like a corpse when he'd struggled out of the back of the cab on Saturday. Today, he looked considerably worse. It was easy to believe he'd die if they didn't take him to the hospital.

The thing was, he couldn't let Mike leave. Crystal would be furious, mad enough to sell him out to Beccs. And maybe even to fleet command. He wasn't exactly supposed to be here.

But.

How could he justify keeping Mike here if he really was that sick? Red's stomach twisted, and he glanced over at Mike.

"No," he rasped out the word. "I won't go."

That solved that problem. Holding him in the bunker when he wanted treatment was one thing, but if Mike was refusing then it was out of Red's hands. At least that's what he told himself, trying to ignore how hollow the argument felt.

"You heard him."

The doctor shook his head. "I'm afraid I don't understand. You asked me to help this man. I'm telling you that he needs medical care."

"So give him some."

Bodhi looked around wide-eyed, as if a medical exam room might materialize. "Pardon?"

Red huffed out a breath. "Follow me."

He led the doctor through the maze of rooms until they reached a supply closet. He produced the key and unlocked the door with a flourish.

"Will any of this help?" he asked as he flipped on the overhead light.

Bodhi furrowed his brow and flipped through the piles of rags, towels, and bandages. He turned to the next shelf and studied the pharmaceuticals. He picked up bottle after bottle, held it up to the light, then shook his head and returned it to the shelf.

"Most of this stuff expired before you were born."

Red grimaced. "Okay, well, he has more cartridges for his inhaler. I saw them in his bag. What else does he need? What would they do for him at the hospital?"

The doctor rubbed his chin. "That's a fair question. His condition seems fairly advanced. They'd give him supplemental oxygen, for sure. And they might give him some medication to keep him comfortable. Look, I'm not a specialist, so I can't say for sure ... but, I'm not sure there are any treatment options at this point. There may be, I just don't know."

"So he's dying anyway."

"Yes, but currently he's dying in a pit. Does he have family? Friends? This bunker's a pretty grim way to go out, Red."

Red knew it. And the knowledge lodged in his stomach like a brick. "Listen, I have to go. I have to report for duty." It was true. He did. After his date with Crystal, but this doctor guy didn't need to know that.

"You're leaving him here?"

"He won't be alone."

Realization lit the doctor's eyes, and he shook his head. "Red, I can't stay."

"Please. Tell me what supplies you need for him. I'll bring them tomorrow. Look, here's a blanket. There's an extra cot in the bunkhouse." He grabbed a thin, scratchy blanket and a sad, limp pillow from the shelf and smacked the dust from them.

"Red—"

"What if he dies overnight? Alone?"

The doctor leveled his gaze and held Red's eyes for a long moment. Red didn't know what calculations and considerations were going through the guy's head. He just prayed they'd lead him to stay. Otherwise, he was going to have to force him to stay and that could get messy.

At last, Bodhi nodded. "One night. I'll give you a list. Get what you can."

15

Red showed Bodhi to the bunkhouse and left. Bodhi made up a bed on the metal cot across from the one that must've been Mike's then drifted back to the plotting room, where Mike had resumed grinding.

He looked up when Bodhi entered the room. "You shouldn't be in here without a mask on," he protested.

"I know. But you need to take a break, let's go rest."

Mike protested feebly, "I shouldn't. I have too much to do."

Bodhi led Mike to his cot, arranged the blankets over his legs, and propped the thin, flat pillow behind his head. He stepped back and considered the set up.

"It'll be easier for you to breathe if your head is raised. I'm going to get you some more pillows."

"Don't bother," Mike wheezed.

Bodhi stopped in the doorway and studied him. "You seem intent on suffering, almost as if you're punishing yourself for something."

A shadow crossed the man's face, and he didn't deny the truth of Bodhi's words.

"I'll be right back."

Bodhi rummaged through the supply closet, grateful that he'd convinced Red to leave it unlocked, and grabbed an armful of pillows and another mothball-scented blanket. When he returned to the bunkroom, Mike's eyes were closed. His breathing, though shallow, was even.

Bodhi laid the blanket on the footlocker at the foot of the cot and gently lifted Mike's head to slide the stack of pillows under it. The man didn't stir.

He settled himself on his own bunk to wait for Mike to wake. As he sat the thought flitted through his mind that he wished he'd grabbed his cell phone from the tent. He could let Devon know that he'd made progress on the cause of the bird deaths. Then he glanced around at the thick cement walls.

Odds were there was no chance of getting a signal in here.

Mike stirred and a rattling breath escaped his lips.

Bodhi refocused his attention on the sleeping man. He hadn't been exaggerating. Mike was very ill. He was deserving of a witness to his life—and perhaps his death. Bodhi watched him sleep, using the silence to observe the man and wish him well.

After a long while, Mike started and jerked. His eyes opened and he struggled into a seated position, gasping for air. Bodhi raised the bottle of water to the man's parted lips.

"Drink."

He sipped the water. "How long was I out?"

Bodhi shrugged. "Maybe an hour."

Mike wiped his mouth with the back of his hand. "And you just sat there and watched me sleep?"

"I meditated."

"Are you really a doctor?"

"I really am."

"What kind?"

"I'm a forensic pathologist."

He watched for a reaction with mild curiosity. Mike chuckled. "Ha. A coroner. Guess this is right up your alley, huh?"

"No. I typically work with the dead, not the dying."

"Yeah, well, you know, I have one foot in the grave."

He didn't contradict the man. After all, he wasn't wrong. Instead, he leaned forward and rested his elbows on his knees. "Which makes me curious about my earlier question. Why are you punishing yourself?"

There was a long silence.

When Mike spoke, there was a hint of fire in his hoarse voice. "It's not punishment. It's atonement."

Bodhi considered that answer, turning it over in his mind like a leaf. "What are you atoning for?"

The man sighed, then shook his head. "I guess there's no reason not to tell you. After all, you're not getting out of here alive, either."

An electric jolt of surprise coursed through Bodhi's veins. "I beg your pardon?"

"He can't let you go. You know too much."

"Actually, I feel as if I don't know anything. I don't know what you're working on or why you're doing it here."

"Doesn't matter. You've seen his face. And if these people are who I think they are, you and I are both dying here."

"What are you talking about? What people."

Mike scrabbled around in his bag and pulled out a mobile phone. He unlocked it, fumbled with the screen to pull up whatever he wanted Bodhi to see, and thrust it at him with shaking hands. "Here."

"You have a signal?"

"Course not. I assume that's why he let me keep it. Look."

His agitation set off a coughing fit. Bodhi placed the phone down on the cot and helped the man sip some water.

"You need your inhaler?"

Mike waved it off, red-faced. "No. Look at the picture they texted me."

Bodhi looked down at a photograph of a woman in her mid-twenties. She had long wavy blond hair that fell loose around her face. Her eyes were wide and communicated raw terror. Half-moons of mascara under each eye suggested she'd been crying. There was a black cloth shoved in her mouth and tied behind her head. She raised her hands up into the frame to show wrists bound together with rope. A wave of cold horror washed over Bodhi as he studied the image. His throat threatened to close.

"Who is this woman?"

"That's my kid. My daughter. They have her," Mike croaked.

"Who has her?"

"I don't know. Read the text. I got it on Saturday."

He flopped back against the pillow as Bodhi scrolled down and scanned the message:

If you want to see your daughter alive again, do not contact the police. There's a ticket in your name from Harrisburg to Norfolk. Leave now for the airport. Bring your grinding kit. A cab will be waiting in Norfolk to bring you to your destination. If you tell anyone, she dies.

Snatches of thoughts pinged through Bodhi's mind: There would be a trail. The plane ticket. The cab driver. The cell phone number.

But none of that mattered now. Not to the man gasping for air just feet away.

"Who would do this?"

"I don't know who."

"Do you know why?" he countered, placing the phone back in the man's open bag.

"Let me tell you a story."

Mike gathered his thoughts, took a careful sip of water, and began, "My father's father, Alfred Hartman, was a first-year student at Dickinson College in Carlisle, Pennsylvania, in 1938. About five years earlier, a group of students in the physics department had begun grinding crystals for the school's amateur radio station. See, they figured out how to use the crystals to stabilize the frequencies. After they graduated, they teamed up with a custodian and started a business manufacturing crystal oscillators and resonators. When my grandfather joined the physics department, a professor got him a job at their company so he could earn a little money on the side, as my grandmother was expecting."

He paused and pushed himself up a bit higher in the bed. As he did so, the pillows slipped behind him. The doctor was up in a flash, adjusting them with a quick, precise movement. For a guy who saw dead patients, Bodhi King had a heck of a bedside manner.

Mike coughed weakly and continued, "It turns

out, grandad had a real talent for orienting crystals. By the summer after his junior year, there were several crystal manufacturing companies in town, and everybody was trying to hire him away, offering him full-time work and a good wage with benefits. But the war was raging, and my dad had just turned two. Alfred wanted the security of his college degree. Then, in December of 1941, his senior year, Pearl Harbor is bombed. Two days later, Alfred's summoned to his physic professor's office. A gentleman from Washington tells him his country needs his services."

"He enlisted as crystal grinder?" Bodhi guessed.

Mike shook his head and tried to ignore the rattle in his chest that the motion shook loose. "No. The man offers him a deal. If he'll go to New Jersey to train the boys at a new crystal grinding school, his service will be deferred. Well, Alfred packed his bags and Grandma Violet and my dad stayed behind in Carlisle. He made a name for himself in the industry. He was especially good at fixing broken units on the fly, teaching the boys how to make do with whatever they could find in the field. A real practical training, you could say. Well, after the war, everybody wanted to hire him. All the big companies, from as far away as Colorado and even

California. He turned them all down and went back home to Carlisle."

"You need a break?"

"No. He finished up his degree and told all the local companies, thanks but no thanks. While he'd been away, Violet had taken in sewing. She'd saved a little bit here and there. With her money from the cookie jar and a bonus from the U.S. Army, they opened their own crystal operation—"

"—Hartman Manufacturing Company."

Mike's surprise must've registered on his face. Bodhi reached into his backpack and removed a small crystal holder. He pressed it into Mike's hands. "Your grandfather made this?"

Mike turned the little brick over in his hands. The smooth, worn case was cold and somehow soft against his skin. "Yeah, this was one of Grandad's. Where'd you get it?"

"It's a long story, and I do want to talk to you about it. But you go on. Tell your story."

"The company did well from the beginning. People say my grandfather had a mind for innovation, and that's true. But Grandma Violet was the businesswoman. Alfred was a hands-on guy, an innovator, an inventor ... a mad-scientist type. It was a family business. Violet behind the scenes, Alfred the face of the company, and their son Joe—my dad—learning at his parents' knees. The company's lawyers set it up so that on Joe's twenty-fifth birthday, control transferred to him. And in 1965, just like clockwork, it did. Violet and Alfred continued to work for Hartman Manufacturing, but it was Joe's baby now. My dad had gotten a business degree, not a science degree. My mother was a stage actress. Local theatre, mainly. He saw her in a performance of "A Christmas Carol" and fell head over heels. I was born two years after Dad took over the business. By the time I was in middle school, he'd acquired most of the other local crystal companies. He and my mom split up when I was in high school, and when I turned twenty-five and he handed the company over to me, it was a multi-million-dollar enterprise and the second largest employer in the county."

"Were you a business major or a science major?"

Mike smiled. "Art. It worked out okay, though."

The doctor leaned forward, rapt. "Really? Even with the rise of technology?"

Mike nodded. "Yeah. I took over in 1992, and soon after, the industry underwent a sea change. Quartz wafers gave way to diodes. Radios gave way to satellites and cellular phones and computers.

Sure, things changed, but everything changes. Those years were invigorating. I got married in 1995 …" he stumbled over his words, paused, and righted himself before going on. "… A beautiful girl. A teacher. She … Laura died in childbirth on our first anniversary."

Bodhi King absorbed that dry fact and all the messy, angsty emotions that went along with it. Then he said, "I'm so sorry. I hope your time with her was a blessing."

And, somehow, those simple words soothed the raw ache that gnawed at Mike even now, all these years later, whenever he talked about Laura.

"It was. Anyway, I managed the company as nimbly as I could. We've remained a player, a niche player in the area of secure communications. A little more than three years ago, I had an idea, something new. An innovation that would do Alfred proud. I started working on it personally, in secret. I wanted to bring a new technology to market, secure some angel investors, and put the company in a really strong position before I turned it over to my daughter in 2020."

"But something happened."

It was a statement, not a question, but Mike answered it anyway. "I started to get sick in the summer of 2019. I tried to work faster, get the project done. It was a true game changer, it would have made the company ridiculously valuable. But I saw the writing on the wall. I was getting sicker and sicker. I didn't want to saddle my daughter with a half-finished pipe dream. And I'd seen what the business had done to my parents' relationship. So a few months before she turned twenty-five, I sold the business to a group of investors. Not the big splash I'd wanted, but a decent sum. Instead of an uncertain future, she got a nest egg. Her freedom. She can do whatever she wants."

"And the investors?" Bodhi asked grimly.

"I never would have expected them to do this, but I assume they're behind this. I imagine they want the tech I wasn't able to finish."

"Can you finish it?"

It was Mike's turn to be grim. "Or die trying."

16

Red raced home after maneuvers to spend some time paying attention to Beccs. He wasn't too worried because he knew that tonight was her hot wives' book club. He waited until she gathered up her book and her bottle of wine and then tottered to the car on her ridiculous heels.

He pulled open the car door and ushered her inside. He dropped a kiss on the top of her head. "Have fun."

She smiled up at him sunnily. "Thanks, babe. I'll probably spend the night at Bridgette's. You know how I get after a few glasses of wine."

Yes.

He pouted. "I'll miss you. But you're right. It's better to be safe."

She waved and pulled out of the driveway. He yawned and stretched exaggeratedly, a tired guy looking forward to an early night's sleep. Before her tail lights had vanished around the curve, he was back inside.

Upstairs, he showered off the grime of the day to get ready for his own night out. Usually, he was pumped up, buzzing with energy at the prospect of a night with one of his "friends." But tonight Mike's papery, rattling cough hung over him like a cloud, and Bodhi King's insistence that Mike was dying pressed heavily on Red's shoulders, a weight he couldn't shake off.

He raked his fingers through his short hair and reminded himself that he was doing everything he could. He glanced down at the counter to skim the list that Bodhi had pressed into his hand. He'd gotten the steroids, he'd gotten the painkillers. He couldn't do anything about the oxygen, but half a loaf was better than none as Pops always said. Of course, Pops usually said that when his mom was crying and bitching about not having enough money to pay the rent. He pushed that memory out of his mind. Tomorrow, he'd take Bodhi King and

Mike their half a loaf. For now, he'd earned a break.

He hopped into the Mustang and barreled down the street, waiting for his baby to soothe him. Even though he opened the throttle and let the machine do what it did best and took every windy backcountry road he knew, he couldn't shake the pall that hung over him. He pulled into the restaurant's lot angry and agitated.

When he followed the hostess into the dining room, Crystal was waiting at the table. Her eyes lit up when she spotted him prowling across the room. She wiggled her fingers in greeting and the light caught the glitter in her dark pink nail polish.

He smiled. She'd spent time getting ready for their date. He could appreciate that; it showed she cared.

"Hi," she trilled as the hostess gestured toward the open seat.

He pulled out the chair and lowered himself into it, placing the napkin on his lap. "You look gorgeous."

She lowered her eyes and gazed up at him through her long lashes. "Thanks. I hope I fit in at this fancy place."

For a split second, he wondered if she knew that

this was always the third date spot. Just how much had she seen on his phone? He nodded tightly and turned his attention to the thick faux leather booklet that listed the wines.

"How'd it go today?" she asked.

He eyed her over the wine list. "Like I said when I called, we're making progress. It's slow because he's sick."

Irritation flashed across her face, but she hid it instantly. After a moment, she exhaled slowly. "What do you mean—sick?"

"I don't know. *I'm* not a doctor."

As soon as he'd said it, he worried that the emphasis would reveal the truth, that she'd realize what he'd done. Instinctively, he understood that if she found out that he'd brought a doctor in to examine Mike, she'd flip out. He slid his eyes back down to the list of wines.

"Red?"

"Hmm?"

"Do you know what's wrong with Mike?"

He kept his eyes glued to the wine list as he considered the question. He couldn't very well blurt out *"it's silicosis!"*

After a moment, he said, "He coughs a lot. He

gets tired. He's real pale, like he's not getting enough oxygen."

"Is he saying he can't complete the project? That'll be a problem."

What kind of problem? he almost asked. But the less he knew about her buyer and whatever the heck it was she was selling, the happier he'd be. He considered the question.

"No. He insists he has to finish, even though it's taking a toll on him. He's worried about his daughter."

"Nobody did anything to his daughter, Red. I swear."

"I know. You've said. But he *believes* she's in danger. He's out of his mind with worry. He'll do what you want because he thinks it's the only way to save her."

He felt the weight of her gaze as she studied him for a moment. Then her eyes dropped to her menu. "Oh—" she began.

"—Listen, let's talk about something else tonight. This isn't exactly relaxing conversation." Thinking about Mike coughing and gagging in that dank bunker made the stomach acid rise in Red's throat.

She giggled, happy to oblige. "Okay. Why don't

you tell me what it's like to pilot one of those big fighter jets?"

She leaned forward. Her eyes shined in the candlelight. She smiled.

Red banished all thoughts of Mike, who may or may not be dying, and the doctor, whom Red had apparently kidnapped, and cracked his knuckles. Then he pressed his palms against the table and locked his elbows. He warmed to the topic and leaned forward to tell her all about it.

Crystal craned her neck to see into the bathroom. The water was running, but she wanted to confirm that Red was still in the shower, soaping away the evidence of their lovemaking. His wife was at her book club meeting, he'd said, so he didn't have to worry about getting home. She'd drink too much wine and crash at her friend's place.

But Crystal imagined his sneaky habits were well-ingrained, so he'd leapt from bed to the shower anyway. Fine by her. She toyed with the idea of telling him that Beccs' "book club" was cover for her own affair with a guy she'd met at the gym. An actual redhead, judging by the glimpse of him Crystal had caught when she'd been trailing Beccs around town to get a sense of her routine.

But revealing Beccs' secret was risky. It could backfire. She'd lose some of the leverage she had over Red if he wasn't worried about his wife finding out. She stretched like a cat then tiptoed to the closet. The deep pink lace of the brand-new floor-length negligee trailed behind her, picking up dust bunnies, lint, and who knew what other horrors from the garishly patterned motel carpet.

She crouched and opened the safe silently, keeping one ear tilted toward the bathroom, listening for the sound of the water shutting off. She cradled the cloned phone for a moment and ran a polished nail over the display like a caress. Then she powered it up and scrolled to the text history. There it was, an exact copy of the text she'd sent from Red's phone.

She smiled down at the image. It had taken forever to get the exact right expression of fear, to artfully smudge her mascara, and then rig up the selfie stick so she could take the picture with her right foot with her hands bound. But it had been worth it. She had the evidence that tied Red, and Red alone, to the plan.

Now if Red would just focus on motivating his captive to cut and tune the freaking galena crystals to specification rather than wringing his hands over his health. He had a cough. Big deal. He'd survive.

Or not, she allowed.

If he really *was* that sick, if he really *was* dying, then he needed to hurry up and get it done before he croaked. Her father had screwed her out of her birthright once. She'd be damned if he was going to do it a second time.

17

Bodhi felt sure that after telling his story Mike would need to rest, but the sick man surprised him by struggling out of bed.

"I need to get back to work," he insisted.

Now that he knew what drove the man, Bodhi understood that arguing would be futile. "At least let's get you something to eat first."

Mike acquiesced. He led Bodhi to the pantry behind the plotting room. Red had stocked it with a canister of oatmeal, some cans of soups, a jar of peanut butter, and a box of crackers.

"This is it."

Bodhi sorted through the cans. "How does vegetable soup sound?"

Mike shrugged, which Bodhi decided to

interpret as a yes. He stepped into the galley kitchen, found a pot, and heated the soup on the aging stove. He ladled the soup into two bowls and opened a package of oyster crackers then slid them across the long metal table to Mike.

"This can't be the mess hall," he mused.

"Nah, probably just where the cook ate when this place was the NCOs' club," Mike guessed.

"Makes sense."

They ate in silence for a while, the only sound Mike's eager slurping. The fact that he had an appetite was a good sign. Bodhi had been worried he might not eat.

"Seconds?" he asked when Mike's spoon stilled.

"Yeah, please. Unless you want it."

"No, it's all yours. If you're going to insist on working, it's crucial to keep your strength up." He scooped up Mike's bowl and crossed the room to the range.

Behind him, Mike chuckled softly. "You remind me of someone."

"Who's that?"

"My doctor back home, Tom. He's been my doctor for decades, and my friend even longer. Tom's a realist. He understands that patients have to do what they have to do, even when it may not be the most medically sound decision. You seem to get that, too."

Bodhi placed the bowl in front of Mike. "In my practice, my patients aren't making any decisions anymore. But I understand the desire to decide your path for yourself even if it might not be the best decision for your health."

Attachment, loyalty, and love were driving Mike to act against his own self-interest. Bodhi couldn't fault him, even though the impulse was likely to kill him.

"You have any kids?"

"No."

Mike nodded. "It's hard to explain, the pull they have on you."

"You and your daughter are close?"

The spoon fell from Mike's hand and clattered against the bowl. He looked down at the table. "No. We used to be. Not anymore."

"I'm sorry." He was. Family dynamics could be painful, for parents and for children.

Mike just nodded.

Bodhi removed the bowl and spoon and carried them to the sink to wash them. "Do you really think the new owners are holding your daughter hostage?" he asked, raising his voice to be heard over the running water.

"Honestly, it doesn't make sense. But nobody else knows about the tech I was working on. So ..." Mike shrugged.

"Nobody?" Bodhi twisted his neck to look over his shoulder at Mike.

"I didn't share it with anyone at work. Except for Crystal, of course." A shadow crossed his face.

"What?"

"Nothing. It's just ... she thought I was underselling the idea's potential. Maybe she was right."

"What *is* the technology? Can you tell me?" He turned off the water, placed the bowls and spoons in the metal rack to dry, and joined Mike at the table.

"At this point, I don't see why not. The market moved away from crystal transmitters in favor of more secure communications technologies. But I don't care how secure your channel is, even if it's encrypted, with enough time and effort, it can be breached."

"I believe it."

"I thought there was a niche for a low-tech option. See, the problem with quartz crystals is that after all this time, anybody can buy a used amateur set and fiddle around with it until they happen upon a frequency that they're not supposed to be able to access."

"So-called secure frequencies?"

"Sure. Happens all the time. Heard about a group of youth scouts that dialed in to the air traffic control stations."

"Huh."

"Anyway, enough scares like that and the national securities apparatus starts running the other way."

"What was your idea?"

"Galena crystals instead of quartz. Quartz became the gold standard in the 1930s and 40s, but before then folks used galena, tourmaline, pyrite, fluorite ... you name it. There's nothing magic about quartz, not really. Shoot, soldiers used to make foxhole radio receivers with a graphite pencil and a razor blade."

"So your innovation wasn't an innovation?"

He laughed. "It was and it wasn't. The U.S. Signal Corps ordered but never used galena crystal radios during World War I. They sold most of them, but there was one on display at the Army Heritage Center, which just happens to be down the road from me in Carlisle. I was visiting the museum, saw it, and got to thinking. I'm friendly with a librarian there, so I reviewed the equipment manuals from 1918 and realized I could modify the design to create a galena radio that would receive a signal at a frequency that no diode on the market would pick up. A truly secure band."

"That would be revolutionary."

"It would be. If it had worked."

"It doesn't work?"

Mike coughed, and his frail frame shook with effort. "It hasn't so far, which is a real shame. The U.S. Coast Guard had preordered four thousand units for their drug interdiction units. That's one reason I had so much investor interest. But when I got sick ... and my work stalled ... they canceled the order and the investor backed out."

"So you sold the company."

"I figured these new folks could bring it to market faster than I could. But I heard they shelved it."

"Then maybe they aren't the ones who snatched your daughter. If the coast guard doesn't want them, why torture you to get them made?"

"Maybe not. But I don't know who else would want the receivers."

Bodhi did. From mucking around in the criminal

mire, he had a very good idea. "The drug smugglers would."

Mike's already ashen face turned even grayer and he pushed himself up from the table. "I have to get back to work. I have to figure this out."

18

Bodhi searched the supply closet thoroughly while Mike resumed his work. He found what he was looking for under a stack of towels. He unearthed two chemsuits, still sealed in their plastic, and checked the sizes. Both were labeled as medium. Good enough.

He dug around, hoping to score some respirators but saw none. He tore open one of the packages and stepped into the olive green pants, then pulled on the matching jacket. He took care to secure the pants at the ankles and to tighten the collar around the jacket, then he found a box of black double-walled trash bags, a metal bucket, and some rags. He tucked the other packaged chemsuit under his arm and headed for the plotting room.

He rapped heavily on the door and called Mike's name. He waited until he heard the whirring of the machine slow then stop before pushing the door open and entering the room.

"What's that getup?" Mike asked, lowering his dust mask and turning in his chair to eye Bodhi.

"It's a chemical suit—an NBC suit, officially."

"NBC?"

"Nuclear, biological, chemical. The military equivalent of a hazmat suit. This one is vintage, but it should still do the trick. I dug it out of the supply room. Here's one for you."

He handed Mike the package. The plastic crinkled as Mike ran his hands over it. He looked up at Bodhi with a puzzled smile. "You know something I don't?"

"That machine, the lapping machine?"

"Yeah?"

"Do you know why it runs water as it cuts?"

"Sure to keep the dust down. That's also why I wear the mask—keeps the dust out."

"Right, well, this equipment may have been state-of-the-art in the 1940s, but I'm guessing that when you were running Hartman Manufacturing your cutting room precautions included more than water and dust masks."

That earned him a wheezy laugh. “You’ve got that right. Computerized filtration system, a fogging system and sprayers that cleaned everything down after each shift. We took safety seriously. That’s why nobody who joined the company under my leadership has developed silicosis. Not like me—or my dad or grandad.” He waved a hand at the machine. “I’m doing my best with what I have.”

“I know. But did *you* know that galena is more deadly than quartz?”

Mike’s smile evaporated and he glanced down at the fine, dark gray dust coating the work table. “What?”

“Silicosis isn’t the only disease you can get from inhaling dust from grinding. Galena is a lead sulfide. Inhaling or ingesting the dust causes lead poisoning.”

“Lead glance,” Mike muttered.

“Right. If you were working with this when you got so sick the year before last, I wouldn’t be surprised if you have both silicosis and toxic levels of lead in your system. Your doctor didn’t mention anything?”

He shook his head slowly, still staring down at the powdery poison that covered his workspace. “No. Tom would have caught it, though. He was thorough, and I had to have a full workup to get on the lung transplant waiting list. He'd have found it."

"Hmm." Bodhi wrinkled his brow. "That's surprising."

"Maybe not. I didn't *have* much galena and it's hard to come by. I practiced with quartz blanks, and I really am pretty good about wearing the mask. I guess I got lucky."

"Well, luck runs out. If you're going to keep working, you ought to take precautions. Why don't you put on the suit and I'll scrub down the room if you can spare a mask for me." He raised his bucket as a visual aid.

Mike nodded and pushed himself back from the table then froze, a stricken expression stretched across his face. "I told Red to stay out of here while I'm running the equipment, but he never wore a mask. It's been a couple hours spread out over several days. You don't think he's been exposed to enough to harm him, do you?"

Bodhi answered honestly. "I don't know. What I do know is he's emptying the trash from this room without bagging it and it's killing the local wildlife."

Mike's head snapped up. "What?"

"The reason I'm here is that the beach across the bay is littered with dead birds. They showed signs of lead poisoning, so I started looking around for the source. I found that crystal holder and ... here I am. Some of the birds are scavengers. They must be going through the trash for treasures and food and picking up dust-coated objects."

Mike sighed. "I never intended to harm anyone —or anything."

"I know. We'll be more careful now. Red probably has much fancier protective gear than this. We'll tell him to wear it from now on. Come on, let's get you suited up."

He took Mike by the elbow and eased him up from the chair. The man seemed unable to tear his eyes away from the toxic particles that covered the table in front of him. A snippet from *The Dhammapada* flitted through Bodhi's mind, unbidden. He couldn't recall the exact wording, but one phrase rang in his head: "evil returns to the evildoer, like fine dust thrown into the wind."

19

It was nearly three a.m. when Red left Crystal's motel room. A light rain was falling, and he turned up his collar to keep his neck dry as he jogged to his car. The Mustang sprang to life and he peeled out of the lot, too fast for road conditions, but not fast enough to outrun his worry. The rain smeared everything in the dark night, making his headlights and the streetlights blurred and streaky. He drove faster anyway.

While he'd been with Crystal, all his doubts had dissipated. But the moment he'd finished, they came rushing back. A hot shower hadn't scrubbed them away. He'd hoped another round with Crystal would do the trick but she was sound asleep, breathing evenly and deeply, when he came out of the bathroom with a cloud of what ifs trailing him.

What if Mike died? What if they got caught? What if Beccs found out about Crystal? What if the Navy kicked him out? What if Crystal found out about the doctor?

He needed an exit strategy. An end game.

His father's words rang in his ears. He must've been seven—eight at the most—when his mom had taken him on the long, rattling bus ride to the prison to visit his pop. Family day, they called it. They'd sat across from one another at a scarred metal table and played chess. Or tried to.

Red didn't know chess, he knew checkers; but another kid and her dad were using that board. He remembered her thick curly hair, the flash of her white teeth when she laughed and squealed, playing with her orange-jumpsuited father. Red and his pop had grimaced at each other over the chess board as they moved the pieces around the board in stiff silence.

Red moved his horse-shaped piece, and Pop exploded. "You left your queen exposed, you dumbass."

Red flinched, but Pop was just getting started. He'd upended the board. Chess pieces rained down on the floor, each one louder than the last, echoing off the cold, empty walls. His mother had wrapped an arm around his shoulder while the guards dragged his old man away.

As they pulled him from the room, he was still shouting at Red. "You'll always be a loser unless you look ahead for the next moves."

What were his next moves here? He didn't know. He wasn't built for strategy. He was built for action, adrenaline. Following orders, rushing fearlessly into battle, and taking risks. Simple.

This ... situation was complicated and messy. He didn't know how to get out of it without pissing off Crystal or Beccs or both and without getting in trouble with the law or the Navy or both. He felt trapped. Just as trapped as wheezing, coughing Mike and that weird, quiet doctor were, locked up in a musty bunker.

He floored it, and the Mustang leaped around the bend like it was alive.

Stay cool. Keep Mike alive until he finishes the job. Once Crystal has what she wants, she'll be happy. Then tell her about the doctor. Get your half of the money and get the hell out of town. Maybe take Beccs back to Key West. Rent a houseboat. Do some deep sea fishing. Make love on the white sand.

The image soothed him, and, by the time he barreled into his driveway and killed the engine, his worries were small and manageable again. They were folded up tight, stuffed into a tiny corner of his mind, and tucked away.

20

Thursday morning

Sunrise

Devon was worried. They'd gone to sleep worried, and woke up worried as the sun rose over the campground.

Bodhi King hadn't come back. The rental kayak wasn't in its spot on the beach. His campsite was empty. Devon had lost count of how many times they'd walked past it. Finally, after dinner, just before sunset, they'd tamped down their guilt and unzipped the flap to peek inside the tent. A fully charged cell phone sat on Bodhi's pillow like a reproach.

They'd slept fitfully and woke from a bad dream with a sinking feeling. They laced up their shoes and walked out to the deck behind the ranger's cabin to fill the bird feeders with nuts and seeds.

If something happened to him, it's my fault.

Devon tried to counter the dark thought.

The water was calm yesterday. The water was calm. The water was calm.

The words rolled over and over like a mantra as Devon sleepwalked through the morning routine of feeding birds, washing up, and walking over to the office. The image from the nightmare was still fresh, and Devon bypassed the office to walk down to the beach.

Please don't let me find his body washed up on the sand.

Drownings were uncommon in this part of the bay, but not unheard of. Devon let out a shuddering relieved breath when a thorough search of the beach revealed no dead bodies—either human or avian.

So where was he then?

The panic that had subsided just a moment before bobbed back up like a wave, threatening to pull Devon under. The loud rumble of a noisy diesel engine interrupted the wave, and Devon turned to see a black pickup truck rocking over the speed bump and pulling up to the pier. The kayak anglers were back. Locals. They were a rotating group of four or five regulars, always led by a blonde woman and a bald man who wore a big hoop earring like a pirate. They were boisterous and rough with one another, pushing and joking, and Devon ordinarily steered clear.

But they'd been out on the water yesterday. They might have seen Bodhi.

The woman and the bald guy hopped out of the cab and started to unload the kayaks from the bed of the truck. A third person, a thin, wiry olive-skinned man hauled coolers and rods and assorted equipment.

"Hi," Devon called out, voice cracking.

The woman turned, her blonde braids whipping against her back. "Morning, ranger."

The bald guy nodded in greeting. Their friend darted into the cab and grabbed another armload of supplies.

"I'm wondering if any of you saw a kayaker yesterday out near the ghost fleet."

The woman and the bald guy exchanged a quick look. The third guy studied his feet.

"Why? What's going on?" the woman wanted to know.

"He went out in one of the rental kayaks and never came back. Tall, thin guy with a mess of curly hair. He was going to paddle out to the concrete ships."

"Thought we weren't supposed to mess around on those ships," the bald man groused.

Devon ignored the complaint and pressed, "Did you see anybody like that?"

After a beat, the woman shook her head. "Nope. Doesn't ring a bell. Hal?"

"Naw."

Devon glanced at the other guy. His eyes were glued to the ground. Finally, he looked up and gave a quick shake of his head.

"Well, let me know if you see him—or an abandoned kayak."

"Will do, ranger." Hal raised two fingers to his forehead like a salute.

Devon hurried away, acutely aware of the whispered hisses the group was exchanging. After one more pass by Bodhi's still-empty site, they headed to the office. After opening the door to the public, turning on the lights, and rearranging the pamphlets, there was nothing left to do but stare at Bodhi King's registration form.

Devon had pulled it yesterday evening, hoping not to need to use it.

It's only been twenty-four hours.

But it's been twenty-four hours.

It wasn't uncommon for campers to leave their sites for a night or longer, but this felt different. The smothering worry was back. Finally, with trembling fingers, Devon picked up the phone and punched in the digits for Bodhi's emergency contact.

The shrill chirp of her mobile phone pierced Bette's sleep. She slammed her hand down on the bedside table and grabbed the blasted thing.

"Chief Clark," she rasped, then cleared her throat.

She rolled over and squinted at the illuminated digits on her alarm clock. Whoever was calling her at five-thirty in the morning had better have a darn good reason.

"I'm trying to reach Bette Clark," the caller said in a wavering voice.

"Well, you succeeded." She wriggled to an upright position and rubbed the sleep out of her eyes.

"I just noticed your area code. I'm terribly sorry to call so early."

"It's fine. What can I do for you?" She eyed the number on the cell phone's display but didn't recognize it.

"My name's Devon Currie. I'm a park ranger in Virginia."

She searched her memory for an interstate investigation involving Virginia and drew a blank. "Okay?"

"Bodhi King listed you as his emergency contact on his registration form."

She was suddenly wide awake.

Her first thought was, '*He did?*' Her second was, '*What happened?*'

"Is there a problem?"

"You could say that. He's ... well, I guess he's missing."

Bette clicked into police chief mode. "You guess?"

"No. I mean, he is. He's helping me with an investigation."

Of course he is.

"What type of investigation, ranger?"

"We've got some bodies here—"

"Bodies, plural?" Her composure slipped.

"They're birds. Dead birds," the ranger hurriedly clarified.

She exhaled. "Oh, okay. You do know that Dr. King is a pathologist for humans, right?"

"Yes, but he's so concerned about the birds. Really, he's the only other person who seems to care that they're mysteriously dying."

That sounded like Bodhi.

"And he offered to help you figure out why."

"Yes!"

Of course he did.

"Did he have any theories?"

"Lead poisoning. But we couldn't imagine where they were getting into the lead. Then he got some idea, he didn't tell me the details."

"So when did he go missing?"

"I haven't seen him since Tuesday night. He asked to borrow a kayak and planned to go out on it yesterday morning. When I did my early morning rounds of the grounds on Wednesday, it was gone. But he never came back."

While Devon recounted the events, Bette tucked the phone between her neck and her ear and located her glasses. Then she padded down to the kitchen to start the coffee.

"So it's been about twenty-four hours since you can account for his whereabouts?"

"Right. Although ..."

"What is it?"

"It's probably nothing."

In her experience, witnesses were the worst at determining what was significant. "Just tell me anyway."

"Well, there are these kayak anglers. You know, they fish off their kayaks."

She didn't, but to keep the story moving she said, "Yep."

"They were out in the bay yesterday morning at the right time, but they say they didn't see him. If he went where he said he was going, they would have."

"There are three possibilities. One, Bodhi lied. We can discount that one right now."

"Why?"

"Bodhi doesn't lie."

"Everybody lies sometimes," the ranger countered.

She laughed. "Not Bodhi. So, option two is he changed his mind and went off in a different direction."

Devon mulled over that one. "Still, if he took the kayak out at all—and it's missing, too—the anglers should've seen him."

"Which leads to the third option. Your anglers lied to you."

There was a long silence. Then, "I did get the sense they weren't being completely forthright."

"What kind of ranger are you?"

"I don't know what you mean."

"At some parks, rangers are considered law enforcement."

"Oh. Oh, no, no, ma'am. I'm an educator. And like a host. When there's a problem, I call the state police. Should I ... do that?"

She considered the question. "You're on the Chesapeake Bay?"

"Yes."

"Tell me which law enforcement agencies are active in the area."

"The state troopers, the local PD, but we're outside the boundaries of the town, so ... not really. Then there's the Coast Guard."

"The Coast Guard patrols the bay?"

"We're right at the mouth of the Atlantic and the drug traffickers have been known to come through the bay on speedboats."

"Anybody else?"

"Well, the military police. Norfolk's just over the bridge and there's a naval installation and the Air Force over there."

The place was practically crawling with law enforcement agencies. "Is that it?"

"Yeah. Oh, no wait. Across the bay there's a National Park Service site. It's not a full-service park or anything. Just a preserve, but it's theirs. So, I guess if anything happened there it would be under the jurisdiction of the park police."

"Hmm ..." An idea was taking shape. But she didn't want to jump the gun. "I'm sure you tried his cell phone, right?"

"No, ma'am."

She felt her eyebrows hit her hairline. "Don't you think you should?"

"There's no point. I popped my head in his tent. It's sitting on his pillow."

Of course.

"And there's no evidence that he's been at the campsite at all?"

"None."

She pursed her lips. "Here's the thing you should know about Dr. King. When he gets his hands on a puzzle, like your dead birds, he won't stop until he solves it. It's likely that he's found a lead and is off following it single-mindedly. He may not even realize how much time has passed."

"Really? So you think I'm overreacting?"

"I didn't say that. I think you're right to be concerned. But at this point, I suspect he'll come back today. And he'll probably have an answer for what's killing your birds," she reassured the ranger.

"I hope you're right."

So did she.

"If you hear anything in the meantime, I'd appreciate if you kept me updated."

"I will," Devon promised.

"Thanks."

She ended the call and stared dully at the coffeemaker, willing it to hurry up and finish brewing. Despite her encouraging tone with the ranger, Bodhi's vanishing act wasn't sitting right with her. It was no surprise that Bodhi would be concerned about dead animals. And of course he'd volunteer to help solve a thorny puzzle—that's what he excelled at. But for all his concern for right livelihood, it seemed to Bette that evil and destruction didn't seep into his world the way he thought. It seemed to her that he went out looking for it. And, more often than not, he found it.

21

Mike and Bodhi drank their instant coffee and waited for Red. Mike had worked long into the night and Bodhi had cleaned up as thoroughly as he could. Now four double-bagged black trash bags sat lined up against the wall on the small landing outside the door. Mike was eager to resume his project but conceded that his aching chest and shoulders would benefit from some pain medication first.

"Does Red always come in the morning?"

Mike checked his watch. "Yeah. Always before seven. Sometimes he comes back at lunchtime with fast food and then usually again in the evening."

It was a risk to leave Mike here alone as sick as he was. But Bodhi supposed that's where he came in.

He intended to tell Red he'd stay voluntarily, so long as Red let him call Devon and so long as Red agreed to stop dumping toxic dust into the trash receptacle. They seemed like reasonable conditions to Bodhi. He hoped Red would see it his way.

The faint ring of heavy shoes striking metal sounded, then grew louder. Bodhi rested his mug on the table and stood. The door swung open. Red stood in the doorway with a baffled expression.

"What's with all the trash?" He waved his hand at the hallway and directed the question to Mike.

Mike cut his eyes toward Bodhi.

"We needed to clean up. This set up isn't safe by modern standards," he explained.

Red smirked. "I don't think OSHA's going to be sending any inspectors out here any time soon."

Bodhi leveled him with a look. "Likely not. But Mike's dying because he spent a lifetime inhaling ground quartz dust. Now, both of you have spent the past five days inhaling lead dust, which is at least as deadly as quartz."

Red's eyes went wide. "That black crystal is lead?"

"It's galena, which contains lead sulfide. The dust is highly toxic if inhaled or ingested. You've been throwing the trash in the dumpster unbagged, you've been walking around the plotting room unmasked. You're as likely to get sick as Mike is."

"I didn't ... why didn't you tell me?" Red thundered at Mike.

"I assumed you knew. *You're* here voluntarily ..."

Mike left the rest unsaid, but Red caught the subtext and jerked his head toward Bodhi. "How much did you tell him?"

"Enough," Mike said in a heavy voice. "What difference does it make? When this is all over you're going to kill him anyway—both of us, probably."

"I'm not ... I don't ... I never ..." Red stammered and blinked as the realization hit him for what seemed to be the first time that most likely those would be his orders.

Bodhi raised his hands in the universal sign for *'let's all calm down.'* "Why don't we focus right now on safely disposing of this trash. Were you able to get any of the supplies for Mike?"

Red nodded absently. "Uh ... yeah. Some painkillers, the cough medicine, and the humidifier. That's all I could get." He rested a brown paper bag on the counter.

"Thank you."

Bodhi opened the bottle of pain relievers, shook out two tablets, and handed them to Mike, who tossed them back with his lukewarm tea. Red was still acting dazed, so Bodhi seized control of the interaction.

"Now let's take the trash out. Mike, why don't you come along and get some fresh air?" he suggested. He was certain the pale, frail man hadn't been outside since Saturday.

Mike's eyes widened and he glanced at Red, who muttered, "Sure."

They trudged up the stairs. Bodhi and Red each shouldered two heavy trash bags. Mike clung to the railing, breathing hard. They made slow progress. But when they emerged from the bunker, Mike turned his face up to the sky and smiled. Tears leaked out of the corners of his eyes, and Bodhi realized the dying man hadn't expected to see the sun again. He rested the bags on the ground and situated Mike on a bench near the edge of the meadow, where he had a view of the water and the trees.

As Bodhi and Red humped the bags to the dumpster, Red said, "How'd you know about the lead, anyway?"

"It's killing the wildlife."

"What?"

"Birds—scavengers, I guess—are getting into the

trash and bringing it back to their nests. The beach across the bay is littered with dead birds."

"Great. That's protected land. Just add that to the list of charges," Red grumbled sourly.

Bodhi tilted his head and studied the man. "I don't understand."

"Understand what?"

"Why are you doing this? I know Mike's story. They have his daughter. What leverage do they have over you to get you to hold a sick man hostage like this?"

Red pinched the bridge of his nose. "You have to understand I'm not a bad guy. I'm not going to kill you, I'm not going to kill anybody. And nobody *has* Mike's daughter. They just told him that to get him to go to make the crystal thingies. This isn't some big criminal enterprise. It's just ... a business opportunity."

Bodhi shook his head. "I believe you believe that, Red. But you're wrong. You're in over your head."

"Yeah, thanks. Tell me something I don't know."

Bodhi narrowed his eyes. "You've seen the picture of Mike's daughter, right?"

"What picture?"

"Someone texted a picture to Mike with instructions to come here if he ever wanted to see her alive again. I saw it myself. She sure looks like she's being held hostage."

Anger flared in Red's eyes. His voice shook as he called to Mike, "You have your phone on you?"

"Nah, it's beside my bunk."

"Don't move," Red warned and then sprinted toward the bunker.

For a fleeting moment, Bodhi considered loading Mike into the kayak and trying to flee. But it was a one-seat vessel, and he knew Mike wouldn't risk his daughter's life by leaving. So he settled next to Mike on the bench.

"What's got him in a lather?"

"He wants to see the text they sent you."

Mike shrugged. "I'm glad you told him to let me come outside. The taste of the salt air, the tickle of the breeze, the warmth of the sun ..." He trailed off and leaned back, giving himself over to the simple sensory experience.

They sat in silence until a crow circled overhead, cawed, and landed at Bodhi's feet. The bird tilted its head and eyed Bodhi sideways. He leaned down and took a closer look at it, then he laughed. "You're the guy who gave me the crystal holder, aren't you? I'll bet you bring Devon goodies, too, don't you?"

He tugged on the paper wristband that identified

him as a paid guest of the campground and snapped it off his arm. He held it out to the crow. "Will you give this to Devon for me?"

The crow turned its head from one side to the other then opened his beak and took the strip of paper in his mouth.

"What are you doing?" Mike asked.

"The crows take gifts to the park ranger. I want to send a message that I'm okay. I thought ... I don't know what I thought."

The crow seemed to understand though. It bobbed its head, and then took off over the bay, wings flapping.

"Did you know that before the Signal Corps got the crystal radio project going, the U.S. Army used pigeons to deliver messages during World Wars I and II?"

"Really."

"Yeah," Mike coughed. "There was an exhibit about that at the Army Heritage Center, too. More than fifty thousand war birds served in WWII, including after the crystal grinding units were activated. A pigeon named G.I. Joe was awarded a medal for saving a village in Italy."

"I had no idea," Bodhi began just as Red raced

back from the bunker and barreled toward the bench.

"Here, show me the text," he panted, shoving Mike's phone at him.

Mike unlocked the display and navigated to his messaging app to pull up the text. He handed the phone back to Red wordlessly.

As Red stared down at the device all the color drained from his face. He opened his mouth and made a keening sound.

"Red?"

"Red, are you okay?"

He didn't answer.

22

Red's mind blurred. His heart threatened to explode. He stared down at the phone uncomprehendingly. Crystal stared back at him with terrified eyes. Her wrists were bound, her eye makeup was smeared, and a black cloth covered her full lips. But that was definitely Crystal peering out at the camera through a curtain of tangled blonde hair.

What was she playing at?

He tore his eyes away from the image to scan the message that accompanied it. It was ominous, threatening, chillingly real. This message had impelled Mike to board the plane and follow the instructions. He believed his daughter's life hung in the balance, and Red understood why.

He tried to rationalize it. She hadn't lied to him, not really. She told him Mike thought his daughter had been kidnapped although she hadn't. This was obviously true—she'd just omitted one minor detail: that *she* was Mike's daughter. He might even have been able to work himself around to being okay with it. But then he noticed the phone number that had texted the photo and the threat. A Virginia number. *His* number.

He flashed back to the first night, when he though he must've left his phone at Wingman's. How she'd slid it across the table at the restaurant days later and said she'd 'accidentally' taken it. He thought she'd used it to catch him in a lie about being married, but it had been something much darker. He choked out a bitter laugh.

She'd set him up from the very beginning. He was a patsy. If this plan went south, everything would point to Red, not her. It would look to the outside world as if he'd kidnapped her or at least forced her to pretend he had. That he'd strong-armed her father into doing this job for some shady buyer. She'd skate away, and he'd be ruined. She was smooth, she was a liar, and she would sink him in a heartbeat.

Distantly he could hear Bodhi and Mike calling

his name. Their voices were faint and distorted, as if he were submerged in water, and they were far away on the shore. He shook his head, pulling himself out of the morass.

"Red? Are you okay?" Bodhi studied him with alarm in his eyes.

"I'm fine," he snapped.

He handed the phone back to Mike. Then he second guessed himself instantly. He should've deleted the text. A second later, he snorted. What would be the point? She'd made a copy.

"I need to leave. So you need to get back inside and get to work."

Mike and Bodhi exchanged a look. Red rested his hand on his holster to remind them who was in charge and repeated the order, more roughly this time. "I said get moving."

He pushed Mike along, even though he knew the man was in no condition to be manhandled. But his anger was building, and he had to get out of here. Now. Mike stumbled, and Bodhi supported him as Red herded them back into the bunker. As soon as they were inside the main door, he stopped and pushed his face close to Mike's.

"I don't give two craps how sick you are. Finish the freaking receivers today. Are we clear?"

"I'll do—" Whatever promise the man had been about to make was cut short by a coughing fit that racked his thin body. He leaned forward and spat a glob of bloody sputum onto the floor.

"For crying out loud—clean that up!"

"Red," Bodhi began, but Red didn't want to hear it.

"Shut up! Just shut up."

The doctor stood his ground and continued in a quiet, even voice. "I'll clean it up. Mike, go sit down. Drink some water. After I clean the floor, I'll help you into your chemsuit. Go on."

Mike's eyes darted from Bodhi's face to Red's, and then he nodded and shuffled off. Bodhi held Red's gaze, unflinching and patient, until finally Red looked away.

Then Bodhi said, "I'm not sure how much you know about Mike's relationship with his daughter, but they've been estranged for the last year or so. She thought she'd take over the company when she turned twenty-five, but Mike sold it. He put the money in trust for her. She's a very wealthy woman, but apparently, she feels—or felt—betrayed."

"What's your point?" Red growled.

"I don't know who she got herself mixed up with, but she should know her father will do everything he can to try to repair their relationship. I get the sense that this goes beyond the threat. Mike wants to make amends before he dies. His daughter should know that."

"Again, why are you telling me this?"

"Maybe you can get a message to her, let her know that," Bodhi said mildly.

Red narrowed his eyes. Did he know? No. He couldn't know.

"I don't have time for this. Just get him back to work. He needs to finish." He knew his voice was more desperate than demanding. He felt close to a breaking point.

"He'll do what he can."

Red stomped out of the bunker, slammed the door, and locked it, trapping them inside. As he stalked across the lot to his car, a thought struck him. He pulled out his phone and opened his recently deleted folder, and there it was. She'd definitely taken the picture—or had someone else take it—with his phone and then sent it to her father. As he got behind the wheel of his car, one thought ran through his head: he was going to kill her.

23

Bodhi set up the humidifier while Mike gathered his tools.

"Will you help me into the suit now?" Mike clasped the chemsuit to his chest as if it were a lifeline.

"Are you sure you're up for this now?"

Mike gritted his teeth and nodded, his grim face grayer than ever. "Yeah, you heard him."

He lowered himself into a chair, and Bodhi knelt and eased the pants up over Mike's boat shoes and khakis.

"That picture of your daughter really set Red off," he mused.

Mike nodded and tried, but failed, to suppress another coughing fit. The stridor sounded worse to

Bodhi's ear; the cough, wetter. Mike was spiraling downward.

"Do you want your inhaler?"

Mike nodded. They repeated the process they'd perfected. Bodhi shook and held. Mike clamped his lips and inhaled on Bodhi's count. Then Mike rinsed his mouth with water.

"Thanks," he said hoarsely. Then, "He recognized her—Crystal."

"You think he knows where they're holding her?" Bodhi asked in a careful tone, not wanting to reveal his private suspicions and compound Mike's pain and grief.

But Mike had suspicions of his own. He answered slowly. "Maybe. But I have a feeling that's not what's going on."

"What are you thinking?"

He shook his head. "No. I don't want to say. If I'm wrong, it's a betrayal of her."

"And if you're right?"

"If I'm right, she's got herself into even more trouble than I thought. Either way, I need to finish these receivers and make them work—or at least make them *think* they work."

From the set of Mike's jaw, it was evident that the topic was closed for now. So Bodhi helped him maneuver into the jacket and handed him a clean mask.

"I'm going make another cup of this lousy coffee and then suit up," Bodhi said.

Mike dismissed him with a wave. As he walked to the galley kitchen, he recalled Red and Mike's reactions as Red studied the picture and Mike studied Red: Both men's faces revealed betrayal, and he was fairly sure they'd both been betrayed by the same woman. He rubbed his forehead. This was the price of attachment, the price of need: it was messy and dysfunctional and dangerous.

He pushed the thought from his mind and wondered whether the crow would take the band to Devon. If it did, would the ranger even realize what it was and what it meant? He needed a miracle, and he needed one soon: In his considered medical opinion, Mike didn't have much time left. Every hour that slipped by, he inched closer to death.

24

Bette did her best to attend to the needs of the citizens she served, but all morning—even as Ralph Morganstern swore out a complaint against his mechanic and Raelyn Loomis filed a restraining order against her cousin—one fact occupied her mind: Bodhi had paddled out onto the Chesapeake Bay and hadn't come back.

She must've picked up her cell phone and put it back down at least a half-dozen times. She argued with herself endlessly. *That tremor in the ranger's voice. The sketchy behavior of the anglers. The dead birds.* ***Something*** *was amiss in Virginia.* She picked up the phone. *He said he needed space. Calling in the cavalry because an adult went incommunicado for a day* *is not the definition of giving a person space.* She put down the phone.

She was just about to reach for the phone yet again when Johansson rapped on her open door frame.

"Come in."

He bobbed his head and scurried into the office. "Here's that report on the breaking and entering at the dairy store, chief."

"Thanks." She took the file absently and tossed it on her desk.

"Everything okay?" He asked.

She looked up, distracted. "What? Yeah, everything's fine."

"If you're sure ..." He lingered in the doorway.

"I'm sure. I have a phone call I need to make. Do me a favor and pull that door closed when you leave, would ya'?"

"You got it." He took the hint, withdrew from the office, and shut the door on his way out.

She reached for the phone, but it chirped at her before she picked it up.

"Chief Clark."

"Hi, it's Devon Currie."

"Ranger, I was just fixing to call you. Did Bodhi

turn up?" She couldn't hide the ring of hope in her voice.

"No, I'm afraid not. I do have an update, though."

"Oh?"

"Yeah. I spent some time trying to figure out why those kayak anglers might be holding something back. You know, what would motivate them to do that?"

"What did you come up with?"

"Well, protocol for a missing boater is to call the Coast Guard, and, you know, speed boats create a wake. Disturbs the fish."

"You think they didn't want you calling the Coast Guard because they wouldn't catch anything?"

"It sounds extreme, but they're pretty serious. They're out here just about every day, fishing."

"Huh." It did sound a bit over the top to her but, then, most people would think internecine feuds between neighboring farmers over herbicide preferences was extreme, too, but that was life in corn country. Presumably, fish country had its own turf wars.

"Anyway, I did reach out to the Coast Guard."

"And?"

"They found the kayak."

"Just the boat? Not Bodhi?"

"That's correct. The kayak was across the bay on the shore of that nature preserve I told you about."

"The one that's on federal land?"

"Yes."

"That's actually good news."

"It is?"

"Yeah, it is. I have a friend of a friend—she's Bodhi's friend, actually—who works as an investigator for the National Park Service Investigative Services Branch. It just so happens that Virginia is in her territory. Why don't I give her a call and ask her to coordinate with the Coast Guard?"

"That'd be great. There's one more thing, and I know this'll sound weird, but one of the crows, Sunny, just brought me something."

"Did you say a crow?"

"Yeah, an American crow. I call him Sunny. Anyway, he brings me little trinkets now and then—a shiny shell, some aluminum foil."

"I've heard of this. Some crows bring baubles to people they have relationships with." She'd read an article about a girl on the West Coast who had a collection of gifts from a crow.

"Right. Usually it's sparkly things. But today he brought me paper."

"Okay?"

"It's the wristband that Bodhi got when he checked into the park last week."

"You're sure?"

"Yeah, it has his site number written on it. I should know. I'm the one who wrote it. And I know he was wearing it. At least, he had it on Tuesday when he examined the deceased birds."

She flinched. "That doesn't seem like good news to me. An abandoned kayak and an identifying bracelet but no—" She caught herself about to say *'body'* and quickly amended it. "—no Bodhi."

"You don't understand, Sunny brought it to me on purpose."

"You think this crow knows you're looking for the person attached to that band?"

"No. I think the person attached to that band gave it to the Sunny to bring to me."

"You're saying Bodhi sent you a message via crow?"

"I know it sounds strange, but I do."

What the heck, she'd cling to that shred of hope. "Okay. I'll pass it along to the special agent at the Park Service."

"Thank you."

"I'll give her your contact information so they can coordinate with you and the Coast Guard."

"We'll find him."

She hoped so. Oh, how she hoped so.

25

Crystal was at the gym—Beccs' gym, using a guest membership to take the barre class that Beccs didn't take because she was busy screwing some ginger—when the text from Red came. She ignored the stink-eye from the woman stretching on the mat next to hers and dug the chiming phone out of her pocket.

Need to talk. Urgent. Meet me at the motel ASAP.

She rolled up her mat and edged her way out of the studio, then hurried to the locker room to shower. Whatever business red wanted to discuss they could either celebrate or commiserate with a quickie afterwards. He'd better have one of two pieces of news: that her father finally finished the receivers or that he was dead. Either was fine with her. Her buyers would be pissed if it was the latter, but she'd figure out a way to handle them.

She was sitting at the faux wood vanity in the motel bathroom redoing her makeup, when she heard the growl of the Mustang's engine. She reapplied her lipstick and was mid-blot when Red started pounding on the door like an animal. She stalked through the bedroom and yanked it open.

"What the heck, Red?"

But he was already pushing his way inside. Fire blazed in his eyes as he kicked the door closed behind him and he grabbed her upper arms.

"What do you think you're doing?" he demanded.

"Get your hands off me," she'd snapped, refusing to show fear.

"I saw the picture on your father's phone."

Oh, bloody hell; he figured it out.

Her chest tightened. She'd dismissed the possibility of this happening as too remote to worry about. Of course, she hadn't expected her dad to take so freaking long to build a couple simple receivers. Who could've known Red and her dad would have time to bond?

"So? I told you his daughter hadn't been kidnapped. Where's the lie?"

"I know you sent that text from my phone, Crystal. Just how stupid do you think I am?"

She didn't care for the way he was snarling at her, so she shot back. "Honestly? Pretty stupid. You think *you* picked *me* up? Please. First, I engineered your little fling with Kathleen because I needed you in a position to get the keys to the bunker. Then I reeled you in. It was so easy."

"What's wrong with you?" He gaped at her.

"So now you're mad because I didn't let you in on every little detail? Too bad, so sad. What are you going to do about it?"

"I'll go to the cops."

She laughed. "Yeah, right. The text and the picture came from *your* phone. You think the police are gonna believe you? And what do you think your commanding officer and your wife are gonna think, Red? Get a clue."

"I'm not going to let you get away with this."

"Yeah, you are." She jutted her chin out and glared at him.

"No. I'm out."

"You're out when I say you're out."

He narrowed his eyes when he realized she wasn't concerned. "What did you do?"

"I told you, I cloned your phone."

"What?"

She said it slowly, emphasizing each word. "I. Cloned. Your. Phone."

"I know."

"Do you, Red?"

"Give it to me." He gritted the words out between clenched teeth.

"Nope."

"Screw you, then. I'll take my chances with the police." He dropped her arms and turned toward the door.

She was pretty sure he was bluffing, but she couldn't take the chance. "Okay, okay. I'll give you the clone."

His eyes were marbles. "Now."

She softened her face and set her lower lip trembling. "It's in the safe. Okay?"

She didn't love the idea of turning her back on him. After all, she could make out the outline of his service pistol under his shirt. So she scooted toward the closet at an angle, inching near the wall until she reached the door.

She yanked the closet open, bent in front of the small safe, and punched in the digits.

"Hurry up."

She swallowed hard as the little metal door swung open. "It's right here, see?"

She reached for the phone with her left hand and pivoted to her left to turn around. As she moved, she snatched her Glock from the safe with her right hand. As she completed the one-hundred-and-eighty-degree turn, she exhaled and was already firing when she came back to face him.

Her Grandpa Joe's words rang in her ears. *"Center mass, Chrys. Always center mass."*

She squeezed off two shots that hit his stomach, then she jerked her hand and the third went through his shoulder. He crumpled to his knees, groaning. Dark red blood splurged from his gut and spread out across the brightly patterned carpet, blending with the mauves and purples.

She stood transfixed for a moment, watching his blood pool. Then she shook her head, tossed the cloned phone in her bag, and snatched her keys from the dresser. As she raced past him, he clawed at her foot. She kicked his hand away and leaned down to fire a final shot and put him out of his misery. But he collapsed as she fired, and the bullet intended for his heart grazed his neck instead.

Her ears rang, her hands shook, and her stomach heaved. She had to get out of here before she puked.

She ran out the door and raced to her car. She rocketed out of the lot and veered into oncoming traffic. A chorus of horns warned her, and she jerked the car back into the right lane just in time, then floored it.

26

Ben raced into Bette's office with a sticky note stuck to his index finger and a triumphant grin plastered across his face.

"Found that number for you, Chief!" The intern slapped the post-it onto her desk with a flourish and was halfway out the door before she could call out a thank you.

She tapped the numbers into her cell phone to place the call. Only after the second ring did she realize that she wasn't entirely sure who to ask for. Probably should've asked young Ben to run that down as well.

"Investigative Services Branch, Atlantic Field Office."

"This is Chief Bette Clark in Onatah, Illinois. I'm

trying to reach Special Agent ... Higgins. Or Jackman, maybe. Aroostine? Rue?" She shook her head. She sounded clueless.

The man on the other end of the phone chuckled and called out, "Roo, you've got a police chief on the line who isn't sure which alias to use."

A moment later, a clear, warm voice said, "This is Aroostine."

"Hi. I'm Bette Clark. I'm the chief of police out in Onatah."

There was a beat while the special investigator searched her memory and drew a blank. Then, "I apologize if I don't remember—have I worked on something with you?"

"No. We have a mutual friend—Dr. Bodhi King."

"Oh, of course, you're Bette! What can I do for you?"

"Bodhi's missing."

"Pardon?"

"He's camping in Virginia, at a state campground on the Chesapeake Bay. Apparently he volunteered to help a ranger figure out why birds have suddenly started dying."

"Is he an expert in birds?"

"No, not so far as I know. But it's Bodhi. You know how he is."

"I've heard some stories."

"Yeah, he can't resist a puzzle. Apparently, he had a theory that the birds were dying because of lead poisoning and he borrowed a kayak yesterday morning to see if he could find the source. The Coast Guard spotted the kayak today at a national preserve on the other side of the bay."

"And, therefore, in my jurisdiction."

"Bingo."

"Anything else?"

"Yes, both points are tenuous at best. Some anglers may have lied about not seeing Bodhi yesterday morning. The ranger thinks they've been less than forthcoming. And ... it's possible Bodhi tried to send a message to the park ranger through a crow."

If Bette could've reached through the phone and hugged Aroostine, she would've. The special agent didn't scoff, didn't question, didn't laugh. Instead she said, "What kind of message?"

"Proof of life. The crow had the paper wristband Bodhi got when he checked into the campsite. Ranger Currie is sure Bodhi was wearing it when he left in the kayak."

Bette heard the clacking of keys. "I'm a few hours away, but I'm reaching out to the Coast Guard now.

We'll coordinate with them and search the preserve before nightfall."

"Agent Higgins—"

"—Roo. Or Aroostine if you want to be formal."

"Roo, then. I can't thank you enough. Will you loop in the ranger, Devon Currie?"

"Of course. Will I see you later?"

Bette cleared her throat. "Bodhi and I are ... taking a break. The ranger called me because I'm listed as Bodhi's emergency contact. But I'm not sure ... and besides I can't leave town on no notice. You know how it is."

There was a silence, then Roo said, "I know how Bodhi is. Not well, but I know enough to understand that he sometimes holds himself apart from other people but I don't think he does it to be distant."

"You met him at a wedding, right? The one where everyone was taken hostage?"

"That's the one. It was a wild weekend. I also worked a case a few years back with his ex, Dr. Rollins."

"I know Eliza—well, through her boyfriend. He's the chief of police of a small parish. We all worked a case together last winter."

"She and Fred are still together? That's fantastic."

"How many people do we know in common?" Bette wondered aloud.

"That's Bodhi for you. For a guy who seeks detachment, he sure is the glue that connects a lot of people."

They shared a laugh.

Then Aroostine went on, "I do think you should try to come East. Just in case he ends up needing you. I hope I haven't overstepped."

Bette made a low, noncommittal noise. "I appreciate the candor. And even more, I appreciate your help. I'll think about it. But you'll keep me posted?"

"Of course."

27

Red's vision faded, going black around the edges like that vignette photo filter Beccs loved to put on her pictures.

Beccs.

He groaned then half-rolled, half-dragged himself to the edge of the bed and propped his head against the dusty bed frame for support. He dug his hand into his pocket, wincing at the hot poker pain that ran up his arm. He took out his phone, hit Beccs' contact icon, and video chatted his wife.

She picked up right away, dressed in her gym clothes. He was sweating like crazy, and, somehow, blood was mixing with the sweat and running into his eyes. As a result, she was pink-tinged, but she'd never been more beautiful.

"Red? What's wrong? What happened to you?"

"I'm dying. I just want to say bye."

"What do you mean you're dying? Were you on maneuvers? Oh my God, Red, did you crash?"

"No ..." There was no point in lying. He needed to tell her the truth now, while he had the chance. "I did something stupid. I was trying to earn some fast money and got mixed up in some stuff. I've been shot in the gut a couple times, my shoulder, and maybe my neck. I can't see it. But I think I'm bleeding out."

"Is someone there with you? Have you called an ambulance?"

She was talking too fast for his fuzzy brain to keep up.

"No. I'm tired, Beccs. I wanted to tell you I love you and I'm sorry I was such a shitty husband."

"Where are you? Red, stay with me. Stay awake."

Her face was right up in the camera. She was talking too loud. He was feeling nauseous. And dizzy. He closed his eyes. "That motel on Highwater Road. The one with 'sky' in the name."

"Horizon Inn?"

"Yeah, that's the one."

"Red, what room? Talk to me."

"Four. No, five? I dunno."

"Okay, hold on. I'm going to call an ambulance. I'll be right back."

It was getting hard to breathe. "No wait." But she was already gone.

He gripped his gut and breathed hard, fighting to hang in until she came back on the line.

"They're on their way."

"I have to tell you what happened in case .... This woman, Crystal, she's selling some kind of eavesdropping technology to drug runners, I think. She's got a guy, a really sick guy, working on the equipment for her. He's locked in at the abandoned bunker over on the preserve. There's a doctor there with him, but I don't think Mike is gonna make it unless he gets to the hospital. Please, Beccs, promise me you'll make sure someone takes him to the hospital. You gotta make sure."

He was rambling.

"Got it. Mike, hospital. I promise."

"And tell Bodhi I'm sorry about the birds."

"What?"

"Just tell him."

"Okay. I will. But you can tell him yourself."

"I'm not gonna make it."

"Don't say that. I'm going to meet you at the hospital. I can hear the sirens. Hear them?"

He strained but all he heard was the sound of his blood rushing, his heart pumping, loud, too loud, in his ears. "Yeah," he lied.

The door splintered open and EMTs raced into the room as Red lost consciousness and the phone fell from his hand.

28

Bodhi thought he heard a siren coming from the bay first. Then he heard faint sirens coming from the land side. He stood stock-still and listened. Definitely sirens, and they were drawing closer from both directions. He stripped off his chemsuit he wore over his street clothes and raced through the plotting room door.

"Mask!" Mike admonished him.

"Someone's coming."

"Red?"

"No. We're being rescued. I heard sirens."

Mike's face crumpled. "No. I have to finish. I can't let her down."

Bodhi made a face and said, as delicately as he was able, "But they're not going to work, right?"

"No," Mike admitted. "The frequency is still wrong. It's close, but it's not there. I think I can make them look good enough to fool her buyer, give her time to get out of town."

"You're not doing her any favors, you know that right? If she rips off bad people, they're not going to chalk it up to a lesson learned. They'll come after her."

Mike shook his head. He was chalk white. "You go. I'm staying."

"That's not how this works. I took an oath to do no harm. Leaving you here would be a death sentence."

"I don't want to go."

"I know you want to protect your daughter, but I think you also know that she's into this mess up to her neck. I can see you want to blame yourself for putting the money into a trust instead of giving her the company, but you didn't make *this* choice for her. She did this. And now you have to make the right decision."

Mike looked woozy, light-headed, and he swayed on his feet. Bodhi could see he was trying to formulate a response. But the clatter of heavy boots against metal and multiple shouting voices took the words out of his mouth. He staggered and went limp.

Bodhi caught him before he hit the ground. An instant later, the metal door banged open.

"Dr. King? Mr. Hartman?" A Coast Guardsman called their names as he ran into the room, gun drawn.

"We need a stretcher," Bodhi told him, still holding Mike up.

"Stretcher!" the man called up the stairs.

Two medics clattered down the stairs carrying a litter. Bodhi lifted Mike's thin body onto the narrow bed. "He's cyanotic, advanced-stage acute silicosis. Suspected COPD."

"Lead poisoning?" one of them asked.

He blinked at the question. "I don't think so."

"What about you, doc?"

"I'm fine. Focus on Mr. Hartman, please."

"All the same, we're taking you to the hospital to get you checked out." A woman wearing a navy blue windbreaker with 'Police Federal Agent' emblazoned across the back in yellow block letters entered the room.

He opened his mouth to argue and then stopped. He looked closely at her dark glossy hair, which was pulled into a sleek ponytail at the nape of her neck. Then he studied her gold-flecked brown eyes. He knew this woman.

"Aroostine?"

She shot him a grin. "Hey, Bodhi."

"What are you doing here?"

"Rescuing you. Bette sent me."

Bette?

"I'm confused," he offered.

She smiled, "I'll bet. I'll fill you in on the way to the hospital. And I'm going to need to you to ID Reid Serrano."

"Where is he?"

"He's on his way to the hospital, too. Although he's in bad shape. They don't expect him to make it."

After the long hours and quiet monotony inside the bunker, the flurry of activity and information was making Bodhi's head swim. "What happened to Red?"

Aroostine cut her eyes toward Mike, unconscious on the stretcher. "From what we've gathered, he confronted Crystal Hartman. They argued. She shot him."

"Is she—?"

"He was armed, too, but never got a shot off. As far as we know, she's unharmed and on the run. Armed and dangerous, as they say. Come on, let's get out of here."

"Wait." He jogged to the bunk room and grabbed

Mike's suitcase and phone. When he returned to the stairwell, Mike was already being carried up the stairs by the medics.

Aroostine put her hand on the small of Bodhi's back and piloted him forward. A thought struck him.

"Is the press outside?"

She shook her head. "Not yet. Let's go."

Avoiding the media was all the motivation he needed. He doubled his pace.

A cheerful Black woman in a jacket that matched Aroostine's drove the SUV, following behind the ambulance that was transporting Mike to the hospital. She met Bodhi's eyes in the rearview mirror while Aroostine made some phone calls.

"Nice to meet you Agent Davis. I'm Bodhi King."

The agent laughed. "I heard. The man who talks to crows."

Aroostine ended her call. "Sorry. That was rude. Flora, Bodhi. Bodhi, Flora. I was letting your park ranger know that you're okay."

"Devon's involved in this, too?" Bodhi shook his head wonderingly.

"We have quite the team assembled. When you didn't return to the campground, Devon called Bette."

He wrinkled his brow in confusion, then understanding dawned. "She's my emergency contact."

"Right. Devon called Bette and also asked the Coast Guard to be on the lookout for you. They found the kayak resting against a tree on the wildlife preserve, which is National Park Service property. So ... here we are," Aroostine said.

Flora flashed a smile in the rearview mirror. "At your service."

"But how did *you* come to be here. Coincidence?"

"No. Bette called me."

The pieces were beginning to fit together. "It's good to see you. Despite the circumstances."

"Likewise. So did you really send a message to the ranger through the crow?"

"I figured it was worth a shot."

"It was quick thinking. How did you end up in the bunker? Did Reid Serrano abduct you?"

Bodhi thought about his answer for a solid minute. "Abduct is a strong word. I ran into him at the dumpster when I was looking for the source of the lead poisoning. He told me there was a sick man inside the bunker, and he needed my help."

"So you went with him." It was a statement, not a question.

"I did. And he was right. Mike was sick and in distress. I told them both Mike needed immediate medical care. Red objected, said Mike couldn't leave. He also said I'd have to stay, too." He turned and faced Aroostine full on. "But that's not why I stayed. Mike refused to leave, and I wasn't about to abandon a dying man. So, while there is no doubt a long list of charges facing Red, abducting me shouldn't be one of them."

She nodded. "I doubt Mr. Serrano's going to face charges, Bodhi. He'll have to face his Maker, from what I'm hearing."

A fist of regret pummeled Bodhi's chest. Flawed and misguided though Red was, Bodhi was sorry to hear that he, too, was going to die.

We're all going to die, he reminded himself. That thought prompted another, and he pulled out Mike's cell phone.

"What's that?"

"Well, as far as you're concerned, it's evidence—

the text that lured Mike to the bunker is on it. I'll turn it over in a minute. I need to make a call."

He pecked at the unfamiliar settings menus until he found Mike's contacts list, then he scrolled the names, searching for a doctor. Nothing. He closed his eyes and replayed the conversation with Mike:

'You remind me of ... Tom. He's been my doctor for decades, and my friend even longer.'

He poked through the list a second time and found 'Tom W.' He pressed the call icon.

As the phone rang, he oriented himself to pick up the rhythms of the outside world. It was Thursday, late afternoon. The middle of the workday. The doctor was likely to be treating patients.

A bright voice boomed in his ear. "Mike, you old SOB, I was just thinking about you! I have news."

Bodhi had news, too. He cleared his throat. "Are you the Tom who's Mike Hartman's physician?"

Silence. Then suspicion. "I am. Who's this, and why do you have Mike's phone?"

Keep it simple. "My name's Bodhi King. I'm a medical doctor. Mr. Hartman is in Virginia, currently being transported to the hospital via ambulance."

A heavy breath. "The silicosis?"

"Looks like."

"Damnit, Mike. Couldn't you hold out a little longer?" The doctor was talking to himself.

"Sir?"

"Sorry. I was going to stop by Mike's place after I closed up today and tell him the good news in person."

"What good news?"

"He's at the top of the list for a lung transplant. The next healthy set of lungs that hit the registry is all his, assuming he's well enough to undergo surgery. Is he?"

Bodhi pursed his lips and considered Mike's condition. "I'm not sure. And more than his physical condition, I'd worry about his mental state. I think he's given up. There's been a ... complication ... with his daughter."

Tom made a noise somewhere between a whooshing exhale and a low whistle. "Crystal. That girl has been a mess for a while now. Mike did good raising her without a mom, but, whew, when she turned twenty-five and didn't get the company ..."

"She's wanted for a long list of alleged crimes at the moment. The big one is attempted murder."

"Not Mike?"

"No. Well, not yet." He could see a scenario

where a prosecutor tied Crystal's actions to Mike's death if he didn't make it.

When Tom spoke again, his voice was hard and determined. "The Hartmans have a cabin in the state forest about a half an hour outside town. That's where she'll go if she's on the run."

"Sir, hang on. I'm going to hand you off to a federal officer. Will you tell Special Agent Higgins what you just said? She'll have some questions for you."

He passed the phone to Aroostine. "He knows where to find Crystal," he whispered in response to the question in her eyes.

Then, as Aroostine peppered the doctor with questions, Bodhi leaned his head back against the headrest, closed his eyes, and focused on his in breath and out breath.

29

Bodhi settled into the molded plastic chair and allowed the sounds of hushed bustle common to emergency rooms wash over him. Out in the hallway, Aroostine paced as she made calls to arrange for an interstate team to track Crystal. Every few minutes, her route brought her past the glass door to Bodhi's left. Mike was in the triage area being examined and assessed by a health care team.

An ambulance sped along the street and pulled into the covered bay area to the right of the patient entrance. Bodhi turned and watched as a team raced out of the truck and ran a stretcher through the bay. A moment later, he heard shouts of "gunshot victim" and the chatter of loud, rushed voices calling out vitals and instructions as the ER team met the first responders and escorted them through a pair of wide metal doors. He caught a glimpse of an IV bag, a man's arm, and a blood-stained pant leg. He recognized the boot hanging over the gurney. And then Red was gone, vanished behind the still-swinging doors.

Less than a minute later, the main entrance doors opened and a young white woman ran in. She clutched an oversized bucket purse. She wore black leggings, a long tank top, a fleece jacket, and running shoes. Her long honey-colored hair escaped from a loose bun. She'd been crying. Her nose was red and her eyes were puffy. She heaved the bag up onto the counter at the information desk and dug out a packet of tissues.

"My husband was just brought in. He's been shot. His name's Reid Serrano. Where is he? Can I be with him?" The words flowed out in a hurry, without a pause or a breath to separate one sentence from the next.

The placid-faced man seated behind a desk handed her a sign-in sheet attached to a clipboard and pointed to a cup filled with pens. "Sign in."

She started to object, then grabbed a pen and scribbled her name. "Here," she thrust it at him.

He studied his computer screen for a moment. "He's in triage."

"Can I go back?"

"No. Not right now. Why don't you have a seat over there? Someone will come out to give you an update when there's something to know." He pointed in Bodhi's general direction and waved a hand at the sea of empty seats.

"Please," she begged. Her lips trembled and her swollen eyes threatened to well over.

"I don't know anything other than what I've told you. Please take a seat," His voice was gentle but unyielding.

She hunched her shoulders and walked stiff-legged to the row of chairs facing Bodhi. She slumped into a seat across and one over from Bodhi. She sniffled a few times as she twisted a disintegrating tissue in her hands.

"You're Red's wife?"

She jerked her head up, a flash of surprise in her eyes. "Yes, I'm Beccs. You know Red?"

He leaned across the aisle and extended a hand. "I met him only recently. My name is Bodhi King."

She gave him a distracted handshake. "Bodhi?"

"Yes."

"This is so weird. When Red called, he asked me

to tell you he's sorry about the birds." She furrowed her brow. "I don't know if that means anything to you. He might've been in shock."

"It does mean something," he assured her. It meant a great deal, actually. But it wasn't urgent, so he tucked it away to think about at a later time.

"Do *you* know what happened to him? He should've been on base in the middle of the day, not bleeding out in some no-tell motel on the highway."

He hesitated, considering how much to share. He didn't want to add to this woman's obvious pain, but he also wasn't going to lie to her. He spoke slowly, feeling his way through the narrative. "I wasn't there, I was at the bunker where Red was holding Mike."

"No, that can't be right. Red said a *woman* was keeping a sick man named Mike at the bunker. He told me to make sure Mike made it to the hospital." Her eyes widened. "Did they bring him in—do you know?"

"Yes, he's here. He's also in triage being assessed."

"Did he .... Was he shot, too?"

"No. He's very ill, though. It's good that Red told you about him and that you called for an ambulance."

She batted her hair out of her eyes and re-secured it in the knot. "He said he got involved in something stupid to make quick money. But it sounds like it was more than stupid. It sounds like he was doing something illegal. Were you involved in whatever scheme he was part of?"

"No, I was at the wildlife preserve for an unrelated reason. I ran into Red and mentioned that I'm a doctor. He told me there was a man inside the bunker who needed medical attention."

"What were they doing in the bunker?"

"Grinding crystals."

"What?"

"That's what Mike was doing, at least. Red was ... guarding him, I guess."

She processed this. "And it has something to do with birds?"

"Not directly. The lead glance crystals that Mike was working with are toxic. Well, their dust is. The birds have been ingesting it, and it's killing them."

"What are you, some kind of bird doctor?"

"No. I'm a people doctor—sort of."

"How can you sort of be a people doctor?" She twisted her lips into a skeptical knot.

It was a fair question. "I treat humans, but they're dead when I see them. I'm a forensic pathologist."

"So you see a lot of gunshot victims."

"You shouldn't let your thoughts get ahead of

you. A lot of people survive being shot," he assured her.

"And a lot don't," she countered.

"That's true. Survival depends on several factors. One of the most determinative is how quickly the victim receives medical treatment. It sounds like you got EMTs to your husband right away."

She sniffled, and her shoulders softened slightly. The smallest sigh of relief. "So, this sick guy, Mike, agreed to grind the crystals for some woman he didn't even know?"

"This is where it gets weird," he told her.

"Wait, it's not *already* weird?" She managed a smile.

"True enough. Red's partner is named Crystal. Mike is her father."

"Oh, so the father was in on it."

"Not exactly. Mike and his daughter were estranged ... how much of this do you want to know?"

"All of it," she answered instantly.

"Think hard about this, Mrs. Serrano. Once you know, you can't un-know."

"I'm sure. Look, I am married to Red. I know he's not a good man."

"I wouldn't say that."

"But I would. Don't get me wrong. He tries. I know he tries, but he had a messy childhood. That's not an excuse, mind you. It's just the reality—he doesn't have a good blueprint to follow for how to be a man. That's one reason he joined the military. But he didn't always do the best job. So whatever you tell me isn't going to surprise me."

"Okay. I don't know the details of how your husband met Crystal Hartman, but I know that she managed to get a hold of his cell phone and somehow used it to send a picture of herself bound and gagged to her father along with a text that said if he ever wanted to see her again he had to do as instructed."

"Cold."

"Your husband didn't know she'd done that. I was there when he realized that she'd sent the message from his phone. He reacted strongly." To say the least.

"Red and his burner phone. He thinks he's so smart, but he's not. He thinks I don't know about it."

"But you do."

"I know about a lot of Red's indiscretions." Her eyes slid away from his. "And I'm not proud of it, but I've had a few of my own. So, Mike comes down here to grind these crystals to sell them? They're like counterfeit jewelry or something?"

"No, they're used to make radio receivers. Crystal arranged to sell these radio receivers to someone on the black market."

"Drug runners."

"Did Red tell you that?"

"It was a guess, but he's probably right. Drug smuggling is a big problem around here. The Coast Guard is always announcing some big bust or another. A lot of product moves through the bay on its way to the Northeast from Mexico."

He nodded toward the door as Aroostine completed another circuit out in the hallway. "Special Agent Higgins will want to talk to you at some point. Anything you can tell her about Red's involvement with local drug runners will be helpful."

She gnawed the lipstick off her lower lip and resumed twisting her tissue.

A tall woman with her hair tucked up under a surgical cap swept through the pneumatic doors behind the information desk, her white lab coat flapping behind her. A pair of dazed-looking residents trailed her. Bodhi's heart squeezed for Beccs Serrano as he studied the surgeon's face. He'd seen that expression more times than he could count. Worn it, too.

"Mrs. Serrano?" the surgeon said in a clear voice.

"Yes," Beccs whispered.

"I'm Doctor Perry. Let's go somewhere and talk."

"Can ... Bodhi, will you come, too?"

He could do this for her. Bear witness to her grief. "Of course."

The surgeon raised an eyebrow but didn't comment as she ushered them past the information desk to a semi-private cubicle out of sight of the rest of the people waiting in the emergency room. The guy behind the desk lowered his gaze as they walked by.

He knows, too, Bodhi thought. *Everyone here knows except the wife.*

Dr. Perry let her in on the secret without preamble. "Your husband sustained multiple gunshot wounds, one of which hit an artery. I'm very sorry, Mrs. Serrano, but we couldn't save him." She glanced at Bodhi. "Internal carotid artery."

He winced. Red hadn't stood much of a chance.

Beccs Serrano wailed, and Bodhi squeezed her hand. Dr. Perry averted her eyes. The residents looked sick.

Red's widow snapped her head up. "Wait. Red is

—was—an organ donor. Did you find his card? Please, make sure you use his organs ... if you can."

Dr. Perry exhaled. "That's very gracious. There's a team standing by ready to preserve his organs if you're—"

"Yes, I'm sure."

"We'll get someone from the transplant center to bring out the paperwork." She jerked her head and the taller of the residents jogged off down a hallway.

Bodhi eyed Beccs Serrano and weighed what he was about to say. But he couldn't stay silent. "Excuse me, Dr. Perry. I realize this is a bit unorthodox, but another man just was brought in. He's in triage—Mike Hartman."

The surgeon looked at that remaining resident, who bobbed her head. "Yeah, silicosis guy. He was being held hostage or something. The Coast Guard brought him in."

"Mr. Hartman does have advanced-stage acute silicosis," Bodhi confirmed. "I spoke to his doctor just a little bit ago. He's number one on the transplant list for a lung transplant."

"Really?" Dr. Perry's eyebrow hit her surgical cap. "What are the odds?"

"Mike is in line for a lung transplant?" Beccs asked, confusion warring with grief in her blue eyes.

"Yes."

She turned to Dr. Perry and raised her chin. "Please make this happen. It's what Red would want."

"This is very unusual." The surgeon frowned.

"Very unusual," Bodhi agreed, nodding.

"Please," Beccs begged, her voice breaking.

"I'll talk to the transplant team coordinator myself. But every second counts. We can't waste a minute," the surgeon walked off without another word.

The resident stammered, "Mrs. Serrano, is there someone I can call for you? It'll be a long procedure ..."

"I have a friend I can call."

"Are you sure? I'm happy to stay," Bodhi told her.

She shook her head and gave him a guilty look. "Like I said, Red wasn't the only one with extracurriculars. Trey will come to be with me."

The resident's eyes went wide and she scurried away, no doubt in a hurry to share the scandalous news with her colleague. Beccs pulled out her phone to text her boyfriend.

"Are you sure you're okay?"

She looked up at him. "I will be. Please, go make sure that Mike gets his lungs."

He nodded. "I will." He turned to leave, and then turned back. "You know, you said Red wasn't a good man. I didn't know him as well as you did, obviously. But despite his flaws, I think he was a good man. He was sufficiently worried about Mike's health to drag me into the bunker, he felt remorse for killing those birds unintentionally, and his last act was to call you and make sure Mike was found."

"He apologized for being a crappy husband, too," she added.

"So, Red's moral compass might have malfunctioned a bit, but I think you were married to a good man."

"Thank you," she said softly.

He gave her hand one last squeeze, then hurried down the hallway to find Aroostine. He needed to borrow Mike's phone to call his doctor back in Pennsylvania and let him know that Mike was about to get his new lungs.

30

Aroostine sat across the cafeteria table and crumbled crackers into her clam chowder. She showed no signs of planning to eat it, focusing instead on firing a steady stream of questions at Bodhi. For his part, Bodhi ate his vegetable stir-fry with the gusto of a person who'd been surviving on instant coffee and canned soup.

"What time does Dr. Workman get in?"

"He lands in Norfolk at four. So, before five."

"Mike'll still be in the operating theater?"

He nodded and swallowed a mouthful of rice before answering. "Yeah. It's a long operation."

"Well, we're in a holding pattern with Crystal Hartman. State troopers are tracking her progress north. At the last update she was driving through Richmond. She'll have a decision to make soon. Either she takes I-95 and braves the D.C. traffic or she goes the long route, which adds almost an hour."

"I think she'll get off the interstate."

"So do I. It's the smarter move for a fugitive. Either way, we'll have eyes on her. There's a team getting into position in the woods surrounding her cabin. The doctor was right, it's remote and secluded. The smartest place to take her from a public safety perspective is to wait until she's alone inside the cabin and move in. Now, we just need to wait. Stakeouts are like fishing, a lot of sitting around, doing nothing—until there's a bite on the line."

"I just can't believe that Mike's daughter is going to end up saving his life by killing Red Serrano."

"The world's a funny place," she agreed.

"Funny's not the word I would use."

"No? What word would you use?"

"Dark?"

She pushed the soup away. "Are you serious? This case has a silver lining a mile wide. Mike Hartman has a second chance at life."

He saw the stiff row of dead birds in Devon Currie's freezer. Heard the piercing cry that escaped

Beccs Serrano's lips at the news that her philandering husband was dead. Recalled the pain that Mike Hartman endured as he ignored his declining health in an attempt to make amends to a daughter who hated him.

"Yeah, I'm serious. Dark."

She shook her head. "What about the rush of having solved a puzzle? Is that a bright spot?"

"Do you remember the case in Pittsburgh, way back when Sasha McCandless was stabbed?"

"Sure, she says you saved her life that day."

"I retired from the medical examiner's office after that because it wasn't a healthy place for me."

"Surrounded by death?"

"No, surrounded by murder. The most depraved cases that came through the doors were the files that seemed to land on my desk."

"That's because you like puzzles and riddles and you're good at solving them."

"That's true. I do and am—but I don't like all the violence."

"Nobody does. Well, most people don't," she amended. "It takes a toll on all of us, but you came out of retirement for a reason. What was it?"

"That's what I've been trying to figure out. Was I just looking for mental stimulation? Did I crave attention? Or is this truly the right way for me to use what talents I have? Is this a proper way to earn my livelihood, bringing closure to the victims of depravity? Maybe it is. Maybe it's not."

She pulled a face. "I know for a fact that you also help the living. Like Mike Hartman. Look, the darkness is out there whether we help people deal with it or not. I think it's better that there are people like us out there, too. But, you have to live with yourself. I get it."

"I guess I have a lot to think about."

"Don't you meditate?"

"Yeah. Why?"

"Maybe you could do with a little *less* thinking, not more." She laughed.

"I have a teacher who calls it quieting the monkey mind."

"That works, too. Do you want a lift back to the campground? I want to interview Devon and see if anything pops out."

"A ride would be great. Is your team making any progress on Crystal's would-be buyer?"

"Not yet. Becca Serrano said Red picked up most of his girlfriends at a bar called Wingman's. He thought she didn't know about it, but she saw his car in the parking lot on nights when he told her he was working. Flora's talked to a bartender there who said Red definitely met Crystal there. So, the working theory is she found her buyer there, too. It's mostly a military crowd, and some locals who fish nearby."

"Fishing again."

"What are you thinking?"

"Fishing keeps coming up."

"We *are* on the Chesapeake Bay, Bodhi."

"I guess." He rubbed his chin. "You said waiting for Crystal to show up at the cabin is like fishing. Boring, right?"

"Right."

"I don't fish, but I've always thought it was a meditative, almost contemplative, practice. You need a lot of patience, right?"

"Yeah. A lot of sitting around and waiting for a nibble. So?"

"So the kayak anglers I met when I was out at the concrete ship weren't patient. They were driven, fast moving, in constant motion. It just struck me now."

She pressed her palms against the laminate table top and leaned forward. "Back up. You met people who were fishing from kayaks when you went out on the bay?"

"Yeah. Hal and April. Why?"

"They told Devon they never saw you."

"No, that's not right. They saw me. Hal's the one who told me to go to the preserve because there's a display about crystal radios there."

"Hal?"

"Bald guy, gold hoop earring. Why would they lie?"

"Devon though they weren't being forthcoming, maybe because they didn't want the Coast Guard out looking for you."

"Because it would disturb the fish?"

"That was Devon's guess. But what if that isn't the reason? The Coast Guard commander who I'm coordinating with said for months they couldn't make a bust to save their lives. It was like the drug runners *knew* when they were coming. They did a full internal investigation searching for leaks and changed their communications systems."

"And did it work?"

"Yep. Ever since they got the new secure radios, they're back in business. They just interdicted a shipment of thirty kilos of cocaine with a street value of over eight hundred thousand dollars. That's small potatoes for coke smugglers, but it was a small vessel."

"Speedboat?"

"Nope. A kayak."

"So, if you were running coke through the bay in kayaks, you'd pay top dollar for a receiver that would allow you to monitor the Coast Guard's secure systems."

They stood at the same time and raced for the exit.

31

Devon quaked in their literal boots and prayed the angler didn't notice. Alex, that was the scrawny, olive-skinned guy's name. Alex seemed to be as nervous as Devon, if not more so.

"But I don't understand, I'm not even fishing right now. Why do you need to see my fishing license?"

Devon coughed. "Alex, we've gotten some complaints about your friends. You know it's illegal to gaff striped bass in Virginia, right?"

Alex's eyes widened. "We don't use a gaffer on stripers. Ever. Not when we're fishing here."

"Really? So you do gaff other places."

Alex forced a fake laugh. "I didn't mean it that way."

Devon's eyes drifted to the bluff where Bodhi sat, hidden in the tall sea grass. How long did it take to search a truck? Couldn't the special agent hurry up already? Hal and April were already kayaking back in. This was all going to blow up in their faces. Devon's knees knocked together.

Breathe.

Bodhi's fist popped up from the grass. Devon exhaled. Finally.

"Okay, Alex. I guess we'll wait for April and Hal to come back to shore to figure out this whole gaffing thing."

"Cool."

The angler turned and walked directly into the path of Special Agent Higgins, who spun him around and pressed him against the bathhouse wall.

"You have the right to remain silent ..." she began.

Devon collapsed on the nearest bench.

After a moment, Bodhi came walking through the grass and clasped them on the shoulder. "Nice work."

"Why's Special Agent Higgins arresting Alex?"

"The drug dogs got a hit off the pickup truck for cocaine, so the Coast Guard got a warrant."

"There's coke in the truck?" Devon's eyes went wide.

"Trace amounts only. But the dogs gave the officers probable cause to search the truck, where they found a bag full of cash and a cell phone that has exchanged texts with Crystal Hartman's number, arranging a transaction."

Devon's mouth went dry. "What about April and Hal? They could be dangerous. They're on their way back."

"Look up." Bodhi pointed toward the concrete fleet as a Coast Guard boat came speeding up the bay toward the two kayakers.

"Prepare to be boarded," an officer commanded through a loudspeaker as a second boat cut around the ghost ships to hem in April and Hal.

Devon watched the Coast Guards swarm the kayaks. As exciting as being part of a law enforcement operation was, it established one thing for certain: birds were definitely preferable to people.

32

Crystal bumped her way up the long, unpaved road to the family cabin, slow and careful. The sun was setting, and the woods were dark. The last thing she needed was to go off the path, careen down the side of the mountain, and end up in the lake.

She was tired. She was hungry. And she was freaking livid.

Red had screwed everything up by getting attached to her father, the ever-charming Mike Hartman. Now she had a real mess on her hands.

A dead partner. She hadn't seen the life drain from Red's eyes, but she knew. There had been far too much blood spurting out of his neck for it to be anything other than a critical wound. A useless schlub stuck in a bunker, dying, if Red was to be believed —although she had half a mind to leave her dad there to die. And a scuttled deal. April and Hal and their ring of kayaking drug runners would be pissed. She couldn't possibly go back to Virginia any time soon, not with a murder charge hanging over her. Besides, they'd only paid her half. It's not like she ripped them off. At least not intentionally.

She pulled the car around back and parked it in the shadow of the big rocks that separated the house from the woods. After she killed the engine, she sat for a minute, regrouping. She told herself she'd figure something out. She always did, didn't she?

She glanced up at the sky. It was almost completely dark now. Time to get moving. Get inside and start a fire. She grabbed her purse and her gun and sprinted up to the cabin. The key shook in her hand as she unlocked the back door. She slammed it closed behind her, then slid the deadbolt into place.

She used her cell phone flashlight to find the switch and turn on the lights. She opened the taps to run the water. Finally she found the kitchen matches and made her way into the living room to light a fire. There was no wood in the hammered copper cradle beside the hearth.

"Come on, Dad!" she shouted to the empty cabin.

It had been a long-standing argument between them, back when they'd still been speaking. She advocated for storing firewood in the holder so it would be there, waiting, when someone came up to the cabin on a night like this. But he insisted the firewood be stored outside because of the insects and rodents.

Think, Crystal. The cabin's made of wood, for crying out loud. You can't leave a stack of firewood, harboring who knows how many bugs, inside for months on end and hope for the best.

She grumbled as she found a pair of boots in the closet and grabbed a flashlight from the shelf beside the front door. Not only did he store the firewood outside, he stacked it yards away from the house on the edge of the clearing.

Same reason, Chrys. The cabin doesn't do us any good if the foundation's been eaten by critters, does it?

She stomped out the door and aimed the light at the pallet of wood. The forest was quiet. So quiet that every step she took crackled and echoed off the mountain. The night was dark. So dark that she shuffled her feet along the ground, taking slow, short steps, afraid that she'd trip over a loose rock or chunk of wood if she walked normally. An owl hooted, a high, piercing cry, and she screamed in response. Her heart pounded wildly and she dropped the flashlight.

Sonofa ...

She bent to grab the flashlight and froze. Its beam of light arced across the ground and lit up the woodpile and one black work boot attached to a leg.

There's someone behind the woodpile.

She snagged the light with her left hand and took off running back to the cabin, back to her gun.

"Runner! We have a runner! Go, go, go!"

Suddenly, the woods were alive with shouting voices, barking dogs, and the unmistakable thrum of motorized vehicles, police ATVs if she had to guess. A megaphone amplified a stern voice saying, "Crystal Hartman, you're under arrest."

She dropped the flashlight to the ground and raised her hands toward the sky. She stood frozen, not moving a muscle, not giving them any reason to shoot her. It was over.

All because her rigid, uncompromising father *had* to store the wood outside. Classic.

33

Aroostine sat behind Devon's desk, talking on the office landline and her cell phone simultaneously. Bodhi helped the ranger bury the birds in the pollinator garden behind the buildings. The sun had long since set into the bay, so they had two floodlights set up on the patio.

"What's going to happen to Alex and the others?" Devon asked, leaning on the shovel.

"They've lawyered up. But from what I gathered from Aroostine's phone conversations, Crystal Hartman is in custody and will be extradited to Virginia in short order. So now there'll be a race to see who can cut the first, and best, deal."

He covered the hole holding Captain with a

shovelful of dirt, then went on. "Your assistance was instrumental today. I hope you know that."

Devon shrugged and blushed. "I'm glad I could help. You helped me figure out what was killing the birds. It's the least I could do."

"Aroostine's going to recommend you for recognition. If you hadn't realized that April and Hal were being untruthful, we might not have connected them to Crystal."

The ranger changed the subject. "Are you still planning to leave in the morning? The site's open until Sunday, if you want to stay a few more days. You didn't get a proper vacation."

Bodhi laughed at that. "I came here because I was trying to work through a decision. I find that I've done that, so I think I will leave tomorrow as scheduled. Thanks for the offer though."

Aroostine appeared in the doorway. "Couldn't this have waited until morning?"

"We had some energy to burn," Bodhi told her. "And you commandeered Devon's office, so we figured now was as good a time as any."

"Thanks for letting me use your space," she said to the ranger. "I'm all done."

"Are you sticking around another day?" Bodhi asked.

"Yeah, Devon's arranged for me to use one of the cottages. I want to participate in Crystal Hartman's interview tomorrow. Do you want to be there?"

He shook his head. "No. I was just telling Devon I'm leaving in the morning."

"Oh, no closure for you?"

"The only closure I'd be interested in is saying goodbye to Mike, but Dr. Workman says he's not going to be cleared for visitors for several days. He tolerated the operation well, but the risk of infection is just too high. Beccs Serrano stopped by and left him a card, though."

They fell silent, staring down at the patch of exposed dirt and the row of neat graves.

"I feel like someone should say something," Aroostine whispered.

"Devon?" Bodhi prompted.

"Oh ... uh ... I guess some lines from William Blake's poem 'The Birds' might be good. Let's see." Devon bowed their head and recited:

She. Yonder stands a lonely tree,
There I live and mourn for thee;
Morning drinks my silent tear,
And evening winds my sorrow bear.

...

He. Come, on wings of joy we'll fly
To where my bower hangs on high;
Come, and make thy calm retreat
Among green leaves and blossoms sweet.

"That's it. It's a duet, I guess, between two birds."

"It's perfect. It captures the sorrow of death and the peace of Paradise," Aroostine offered.

They both turned and stared at her.

"English major," she explained, ducking her head.

"On that note, I'm going to turn in. It's been an exciting day, to say the least." Bodhi shook Devon's hand and then Aroostine's.

"You can do better than that." She feigned offense, and then hugged him. "Tell Bette I said hi."

At least that's what it sounded like. He must be more tired than he realized.

"Pardon?"

"Good night."

"Oh, good night."

Bodhi trudged to his campsite, yawning widely. He hadn't been exaggerating. It had been a long day—two days, actually. He was looking forward to drinking a mug of tea while he gazed up at the stars and then crawling into his tent and sleeping.

"It's about time," a familiar husky voice drawled. "The Lyrids has already started. You're missing the fireballs."

"Bette?"

His clicked on his flashlight and illuminated the front of his tent.

"Over here."

He shifted the light. Bette sat in a camping chair to the left, her trusty blue travel mug in her hand. A second chair was set up next to hers. She stood and handed him his camping mug. He sniffed and inhaled the scents of ginger and turmeric. His end of the day tea.

"What are you doing here?"

"The new moon was only a few days ago, so the night sky's still pretty amazing. And the meteor showers are peaking. I figured this was as good a place as any to watch them."

He rested his mug on the picnic table then gently pried hers out of her hand. "Seriously, Bette."

She sighed. "Seriously, Bodhi. I spoke to Aroostine, and it sounds like your restful camping trip turned out to be fairly harrowing between the poisoned birds, the dying man, the abduction, the murder, and the drug smugglers. Thought you might like to see a friendly face."

"Well, when you put it like that, it does sound like the world's worst vacation."

She laughed. "It definitely makes the short list." Her smile faded. "But, if you'd rather be alone, that's okay, too. Aroostine has an extra bed in her cottage, and I can bunk with her."

He switched off the flashlight, grabbed the mugs, and led Bette over to the chairs. "No. I'm glad you're here. There's nobody I'd rather look for shooting stars with than you."

They settled into their seats, tipped their heads back, and sipped their tea in silence.

After a long moment, she said, "Did you figure out anything about your livelihood?"

He nodded even though she couldn't see him in the dark. "Yeah. I realized '*there is nothing either good or bad, but thinking makes it so.*'"

"Did the Buddha say that?"

"No, William Shakespeare wrote it. It's from *Hamlet.*"

"You're quoting Shakespeare now?"

"I was hanging around with an English major all day. Don't worry, the effects should wear off."

Bette laughed lightly. Then, "What's it mean—to you?"

"I guess I mean that if I look for darkness, death, and depravity, then that's what I'll find, and I won't feel that my work fulfills the requirements for right livelihood. But if I look for the closure and healing and justice my work brings, then that's what I'll find."

"Closure, healing, and justice sure sound like an honorable way to earn a living."

"Agreed."

They looked back up at the sky. After a moment, a bright blur streaked overhead.

"Did you see that one?"

She grabbed his arm. "To your left, look, another one!"

The meteors were shooting faster now. He watched as one brilliant light prick after another zipped across the purple sky. He filled his lungs with the crisp air and listened to the night songs of the katydids and crickets. He sipped his fragrant tea. He rested his hand on Bette's arm, feeling the warmth of her skin radiating even through her thin jacket.

"I'm glad you're here."

AUTHOR'S NOTE

Long-time readers know I often find inspiration for my books from places my family has visited. Last year, the plan was to take a six-week RV trip to explore Utah. I could just imagine all the plot bunnies, ideas, and twists I'd discover along the way.

And, then came COVID. Our trip was canceled, and the RV stayed in storage for most of 2020. In late September, we made a short trip to a state park in Virginia. It was a strange visit. The park was mostly empty, lots of exhibits and activities were canceled, and we eschewed our usual exploration of local restaurants. But our hikes, walks, and explorations were a welcome change of pace and the surroundings were gorgeous.

And, sure enough, during one of our walks on the beach, the seed of the idea for *Flight Path* revealed itself to me! The park where we stayed, Kiptopeke State Park, is smack in the middle of the Atlantic Flyway, and we saw loads of migrating birds and butterflies. It's also home to the Ghost Fleet of Kiptopeke, nine partially sunken concrete ships that form a breakwater just off the beach.

Birds, ghost ships, and the World War II bunker we stumbled across during a walk through a nearby wildlife and nature preserve stayed with me long after we returned home and came together to inspire *Flight Path.* Properly inspired, I started my research. As many of you know, my Bodhi King books are some of my most research-intensive titles.

This time around, I learned about the U.S. Army Signal Corps.' Pigeon Service, lead poisoning in birds, silicosis in people, the history of crystal grinding in Carlisle, PA (right down the road from me!), and more about crystal radio and the U.S. Signal Corps.' crystal grinding program than I could possibly ever need to know!

I doubt many (any?) of you will want to read an entire book or a multi-volume military history about crystal grinders (but, hey, if you do, send me an email and I'll share loads of links), so here's a vintage documentary, entitled "Crystals Go to War," for your viewing enjoyment: https://archive.org/details/6101_Crystals_Go_to_War_01_20_16_21 And I also read a genuinely fascinating book, *The Genius of Birds*, for background but exactly none of what I read made it into *Flight Path*. Perhaps it will find its way into the pages of a future book, perhaps not. Either way, I have a greater appreciation for the birds I see out and about. I highly recommend this book!

THANK YOU!

Thanks for reading *Flight Path!* Bodhi will be back in another adventure soon. While you wait, you can always find an up-to-date list of the titles in this series, as well as my other books, on my website, www.melissafmiller.com.

Sign up. To be the first to know when I have a new release, sign up for my email newsletter. Prefer text alerts? Text BOOKS to 636-303-1088 to receive new release alerts and updates. Subscribers receive new release alerts, notices of sales and other book news, goodies, and exclusive subscriber bonuses.

Keep reading. Check out the first book in one (or all) of my other three series:

Irreparable Harm (Sasha McCandless Legal Thriller No. 1):

Sasha's a five-foot nothing attorney who's trained in Krav Maga. She's smart, funny, and utterly fearless. More than one million readers agree: you wouldn't want to face off against her in court ... or in a dark alley.

Critical Vulnerability (Aroostine Higgins Thriller No. 1):

Aroostine relies on her Native American traditions and her legal training to right wrongs and dispense justice. She's charmingly relentless, always dots her *i*'s and crosses her *t*'s, and is an expert tracker.

Rosemary's Gravy (We Sisters Three Humorous Romantic Mystery No. 1):

Rosemary, Sage, and Thyme are three twenty-something sisters searching for career success and love. Somehow, though, they keep finding murder and mayhem ... and love.

Share it. If you liked this book, please lend your copy to a friend who might enjoy it.

Review it. Please consider posting a short review. Honest reader reviews help others decide whether they'll enjoy a book.

ALSO BY MELISSA F. MILLER

The Sasha McCandless Legal Thriller Series

Irreparable Harm

Inadvertent Disclosure

Irretrievably Broken

Indispensable Party

Lovers and Madmen (Novella)

Improper Influence

A Marriage of True Minds (Novella)

Irrevocable Trust

Irrefutable Evidence

A Mingled Yarn (Novella)

Informed Consent

International Incident

Imminent Peril

The Humble Salve (Novella)

Intentional Acts

In Absentia

Inevitable Discovery

Full Fathom Five (Novella)

The Aroostine Higgins Novels

Critical Vulnerability

Chilling Effect

Calculated Risk

Called Home

Crossfire Creek

Clingmans Dome

The Bodhi King Novels

Dark Path

Lonely Path

Hidden Path

Twisted Path

Cold Path

Flight Path

Shehandoah Shadows Novella Series

Burned

Scorched

Ablaze

The We Sisters Three Romantic Comedic Mysteries

Rosemary's Gravy

Sage of Innocence

Thyme to Live

Lost and Gowned: Rosemary's Wedding

Wedding Bells and Hoodoo Spells: Sage's Wedding

Wanted Wed or Alive: Thyme's Wedding

Made in the USA
Las Vegas, NV
18 March 2022